What people are saying

Jamie Lisea has the modern gift of story telling--from very contemporary "business-talk" in high-rise downtown to "down-home" Latino family-talk on the other side of town, and real human living places in between. I warmly recommend her book!

Frederick Dale Bruner

Author of commentaries on the Gospels of Matthew and John, and of

A Theology of the Holy Spirit

What would the gospel story look like if it happened in our time? Now we know. In Jamie Lisea's re-imagining, the old story becomes fresh and new. She has an uncanny gift for getting inside the heart of the prodigal son, the rich young ruler, and the woman at the well. As we follow her retelling of their encounters with Jesus in terms of our present time, we suddenly find that we are in the presence of Jesus, just as they were.

Dr. G. Walter Hansen

Author of *Abraham in Galatians, Galatians* (IVP Commentary Series), and

The Letter to the Philippians

A brave writer presenting contemporary images of Jesus, Jamie Lisea has a gift for asking compelling questions that arise from the interactions with Jesus made live for us today in our world. These stories make you willing to ask, "What if I were there today? What would my response to Jesus be amidst that kind of intensity?" Her writing touches our areas of vulnerability and helps us land in a fresh place of courageous belief.

Ann Shackelton

Young Life Senior Vice President, and Marriage and Family Therapist

Jamie Lisea has beautifully touched the 'universal ache' which all of us have - deep down in our gut, and she has sensitively addressed its depth . . . its loneliness . . . and its potential healing. These are great stories. It made me realize again why the Greatest Teacher in History both told and was a part of so many stories like these.

Barton Tarman

International speaker, Minister-at-large for the Presbyterian Church, former Chaplain of Westmont College

Few things make Bible truths come alive like putting them in modern day settings. Jamie Lisea has done just that as she retells Jesus' encounter with the rich young ruler, the woman at the well, and His own parable of the lost son.

Bill Myers

Author of *Child's Play*

Jesus told and lived stories in the first century. Each of us is living a story in the 21st century. These stories by Jamie Lisea connect our stories with the Jesus story in terms that are creative, passionate, and often earthily raw. The Jesus that is so real and alive to her becomes real and alive to us in these marvelously told stories . . . and nothing is more important.

Howard Baker

Assistant Professor of Christian Formation, Denver Seminary

Author of *Soul Keeping: Ancient Paths of Spiritual Direction*

Jamie Lisea is a treasure. I highly recommend her book for two reasons. First, it will pierce your heart and help you touch thoughts and emotions you may have missed or avoided. Second, is because these words are penned by a woman who has lived her faith courageously and relationally for a number of years. Her wisdom is real and hard earned. Trust her. In these stories, she has captured not only scriptural truths but she has brought them to life in a beautiful way. Do yourself a favor. Read this book.

Dr. Larry Anderson
Senior Pastor, North Bible Church

Jamie Lisea captures the heart of Jesus' stories, and combines it with the realism of contemporary culture. Her writing draws you in with just the right amount of description and emotion to trigger your biblical memory, and connect to where you are.

Laurie Polich Short
Speaker, author, associate pastor

RICH
THIRSTY
HUNGRY

and the freedom that finds us there

Jamie Lisea

Rich Thirsty Hungry

ISBN: 978-0-9911655-0-6

Cover design by Hillary Hope of The Unlimited Hope, Inc.
Cover photograph by Phillip Van Nostrand

For my boys, who bring me such great joy.
I love who each of you are becoming.

For my friends and family, who love me, support me,
and send me.

For Scott, who teaches me the most
about being loved and loving.

And for the Source of this love, who began
this whole thing in the first place.

I'm so deeply grateful.

Contents

Introduction

Whether we've learned about him because we're amused, or see him as one of many good spiritual teachers, or believe him to be God, we share in common that Jesus has held our attention for thousands of years. In addition to the lessons he taught, perhaps just as beloved are his stories and his interactions with people. They're wonderful and amazing stories of love and freedom.

Love and freedom: Aren't these spectacular words?

When love and freedom enter a story, the opportunity for tremendous change begins. The stories of Jesus are full of these opportunities, and are as relevant today as when they first happened centuries ago.

However . . .

To many of us, they don't feel that way. They seem archaic. The language seems confusing. Sometimes the lessons and values can feel too narrow, confining, or outdated. Or, we've heard them so many times that we tune them out. And sometimes they're just not all that interesting to us.

But . . .

What if we could pull these encounters forward into our life now? What if Jesus were walking in your city today and meeting someone for coffee, doing some work on his computer, coaching your kids' soccer team, surfing with friends and then having a bonfire with drinks and burgers? Do you wonder how his conversations with people would sound . . . today? Would they be different? What would you think of him if you bumped into him on the street? Have you ever wondered that?

Jesus said that all things are possible. The following stories speak to this hope and the belief that if Jesus were with us today, the meaningful moments between him and others would be as powerful as they were originally. He would get our attention. We would notice something different.

This is the hope of this book: By bringing one story that Jesus told and two encounters that Jesus had with people into the modern day, the characters, settings, and language can give us a fresh place from which to wonder and engage, and possibly even to experience love and freedom at a depth we've not yet experienced before.

Could there be more for us in these stories? This is a possibility worth wondering about.

RICH
THIRSTY
HUNGRY

and the freedom that finds us there

The Long Road

Prologue

Now all the people working for great profit; those charging enormous prices to make money for themselves by taking advantage of others; those who partied wildly without morals or shame; those who abused women and children; those who gossiped and lied to make themselves look good; those who cheated their way to winning at whatever they wanted; those who sold and engaged in pornography; those who stripped the land of its resources at the expense of the impoverished people living there; those who hated freedom; those who killed to make a change; and many others were coming near him and listening to him. They were drawn to him. They'd never heard anyone speak this way. He gave them hope. The definitions they'd always heard and been taught were different. They began to think that there might be a place for them, and they began to wonder about a different way to live.

And the religious and reputable people, those who followed the rules, those who felt the responsibility to keep themselves and others in line, those who really tried, and those whose life seemed to "work" for them, began to get mad and to complain, "This man receives the dishonest, the partiers, the abusers, the liars, the cheaters, the immoral, the greedy, the terrorists, and the outsiders." They were disgusted and didn't know why he would do such a thing. His words and actions, offered to the others, seemed to make light of their serious pursuit to live honorably.

And so, he told them this tale.

What I remember most about that day was my thirst. It was the type of thirst that sneaks up on you, becomes more and more noticeable, and then has your full attention. Then came the nausea, and I recognized in an instant that I was going to be sick. With the crowd of people around me, I panicked at the scene in my mind that I could see play out. *I'm going to throw up in front of everyone. No! God, no!* Before I could help it, I lost it right there, in the middle of my estranged family and friends and a crowd that seemed to be about three or four hundred people, many of whom I knew growing up: teachers, neighbors, families, friends, my boss from my first job, my high school baseball coach, they all seemed to be there. There was nowhere to hide and nowhere to recover from the humiliation.

It was an upheaval like I've never had before, and it seemed to go on and on. The scourging was thorough. It was more than the previous meal. It was fear and guilt and shame. It was pain and embarrassment. It was all of my insides, stored and coddled for years, spewed up for all to see. I was doubled over and couldn't look up out of embarrassment and utter exhaustion.

✳

Actually, this is where my road ended. The pain had begun about 15 years earlier. This is a story about me and my journey that concluded in this scene, which turned out to be in the middle of a reception, about five yards away from an amazingly beautiful cake.

It all began when I was becoming a teenage boy, when many journeys begin to take shape and decisions are made to enter roads and paths, which often lead to very unfortunate destinations. Such was my story.

I didn't know it then, but as I look back, I was making some decisions, a couple in particular, long before they showed up in my life. And these decisions drove some stakes into what I would become. They were lines that I would not cross and ideas that I would live by.

The first decision was about being alone. For the first 12 years of my life, my family may have looked pretty normal, whatever that is. My mom worked for the county newspaper, selling advertisement to local businesses.

She threw great parties, especially birthday parties for us kids. My 10th birthday, "Football Party," was my favorite. My dad was supposed to be dressed as Joe Montana, my favorite 49er player, but he was delayed at work that afternoon. Just after the chorus of "Happy Birthday," my mom spontaneously burst into the room in full pads and gear, and blackout under her eyes. My friends loved it, and I loved her.

That is my favorite childhood memory of her. Her deep brown eyes and scattered honey blonde hair were as warm as the hugs she gave me each time I needed one.

My father was an engineer of some things that I've never really been able to understand, but I knew that he was smart. He was part of a group at MIT as a graduate student, and they discovered some theory that has become important in aerospace technology, which made us comfortable, I guess you could say. We had a big house, nice cars, and took great vacations.

I have an older brother by three years, Ben, who I remember as being distant and good at everything he tried growing up. "Ben, you are so responsible," I once overheard a neighbor say, as she was paying him for taking care of their house one summer while their family was traveling. I could see his face across the yard from where I was raking leaves for my dad, and his expression and posture held something new to me. He straightened his shoulders back, and held his chin forward with a big, proud smile. There was no question in my mind that this made Ben feel like he could walk the moon. And I have always thought that he could.

My younger sister, Julia, was quiet and beautiful, but I didn't know her much because she was five years younger than me. Early on in our childhood, Julia got sick and had to be in the hospital for a couple of weeks. Her pale face and slight, sweet smile were all the color that hospital room had to offer, that and the warmth of her hand when she reached out to hold mine.

We all wanted to protect her after that.

✳

One day, a few months after my 12th birthday and a
few days after school got out for the summer, my dad came
home really late from work. Julia and I were in bed, but I
wasn't asleep yet. It was warm that night. I was laying on top
of the covers in my shorts, drifting in thought to a tree house I
wanted to build in one of our backyard oaks.

*Three solid walls, with a window on each side, and a door
made from the wood on the side of our house. I'll paint it brown and
green camouflage on the outside and maybe black on the inside...*

It was an unusual night because my mom hadn't come
home in the afternoon like normal and hadn't called either.
My brother was home and watched over me and Julia like he
had done a lot anyway, so I hadn't really thought about it
much other than I wished my mom would've been home so
that Ben wasn't in charge. He was usually doing his own thing
and didn't pay much attention to us.

I heard a bowl being scraped by a spoon, looking for
anything left. *That's his second helping of ice cream!* The
national news was playing in the background, covering a story
of a military rescue somewhere in Africa of some former
terrorist. People were outraged at the "atrocity," is what I
heard. *What does "atrocity" mean? What exactly is a "terrorist"?* I
remember thinking. It was a familiar word, but I hadn't really

paid attention to what they were mad about or who exactly they wanted to kill.

I heard the door open and heard my dad throw his keys down in the bowl by the front door that our family had brought home from a trip to Hawaii, with palm trees painted on it. I heard him walk into the kitchen and heard my brother say, "Hi Dad." I didn't hear his response but heard my brother's voice again, "Dad, you alright?" I got curious and got out of bed. When I turned the corner into the kitchen, I saw my Dad just as he was reaching out to hug my brother, and he began to cry. My brother looked at me confused. I ran over and hugged them, and said, "What's wrong? What's wrong, Dad? Where's Mom? Is she alright?"

He was shaking. His face was contorted in such a way that it was hard to recognize him. His arms seemed endlessly long as they opened up and surrounded us both. His fingers slowly dug into one of my shoulders, and I wincingly tried to match his grip, almost as if I were trying to hold him up and keep him from falling. One of his pockets of his pants was unusually inside out, and it looked like water stains were on his pant legs as I looked down and continued my squeeze.

What followed was something I'd never considered about Mom, never in a million years.

She had left us.

When my dad first said this, I couldn't fathom what he even meant. *Left for where?*

She had some close college friends, Auntie Carol,

Auntie Liz, and Auntie Jo, whom she spent one or two weekends with a year. They were considered part of our family. *She probably went to be with them and didn't get it on the calendar.*

She went to a convention with work each year in Las Vegas. *It had just been a few months ago, but she probably got invited to another one last minute and neglected to tell Dad.*

But through my dad's tears, it became painfully obvious that she had left to nowhere in particular . . . but had left . . . us.

I thought that I was really close to her, and I thought that she understood me more than anyone else in our family. We used to sit on the back porch on Saturday mornings and play tic-tac-toe with sidewalk chalk and drink chocolate milk. "Jacob, you're so fun to be with," I could hear her say.

I felt so stupid. I felt ashamed: like I was nothing.

＊

From there, my dad's life, and therefore all of our lives, really suffered for a long time. Aunt Cindy, my Mom's sister, stepped in to help us out. I always wondered if she felt guilty about it or something. A lot of times, even though she tried hard, she seemed angry – and as time went on, she seemed to be angry with my mom and with us. Whenever her name came up or she was referred to, it seemed Cindy's expression changed, and she became impatient.

While doing the dishes together one night after dinner, I dropped a plate in the sink and it shattered. I looked up at her, and she began to cry and then tossed the towel down and walked out of the room. "I'm just tired Jacob; it's not your fault," she said when she left that night.

My dad struggled to make things work for us. He tried to work shorter hours so that he could be home earlier and be more involved in our lives. He went to all of our events that he could, often skipping his lunch hour to get to a conference with a teacher or to drive us to a doctor's appointment. He stayed at home with us when we were sick.

One time, I remember him canceling some kind of important meeting when Julia had a fever and was staying home from school. He must have caught some heat for this, because I took a message that afternoon from a frustrated colleague of his, who harshly said, "Tell him they dropped the project!" and hung up.

Sometimes, I would hear him cry late at night. And it made me sad and then mad for some reason. It was miserable and pathetic. *Maybe Mom left him because he wasn't strong enough. Maybe he did something really bad to her.* I didn't like to hear him cry.

And so I decided, on one of those nights, something that would stay with me for years to come: that I would not be alone in my life, whatever it took. No matter what, I would not be lonely.

✳

A few years later, my dad was driving home from work, trying to catch one of my baseball games, and was hit by someone who ran a stop sign.

It was the 5th inning, and our game was tied 3-3. I was playing third base, ready for a hit from the batter, who had driven a ball at me three innings earlier. The sirens were faint at first and then grew near, to the point where the umpire behind the plate called timeout.

There was a grassy knoll behind home plate, and we all saw the officer walking over it toward the field. He walked over to my coach and spoke with him quietly. We were throwing a ball around in the infield to stay warm.

Where's my Dad? He should've been here by now.

My heart sank as the coach quickly glanced at me. *Oh no, God.* He listened some more, nodded, and then called the team off the field. When he started talking with the team and put his hand on my shoulder, I knew it was about me.

The game was called, and my coach drove me to the hospital where Ben, Julia, and my Aunt Cindy were already waiting. The surgery went well into the night. We watched the late night news in the waiting room, which covered my dad's accident. We watched with surreal fascination, wanting to see it while wanting to look away, much like a horror movie. Apparently, an elderly woman ran the stop sign and was in stable condition. The site of the car, metal crumpled and squeezed into the driver's seat as if recycled aluminum, made Julia get up and run out of the room crying with Aunt Cindy following after her.

We waited and waited, until I couldn't stay awake any longer and began to fall asleep lying across several chairs. As I drifted off, I noticed the grass stains on my knees, and I wished that I could be back on that field, before all of this happened.

Aunt Cindy nudged me awake, just as I saw the doctor leaving the waiting room. It was still dark outside. Julia was still asleep, but Ben was sitting in a chair across from me, his face in his hands over his knees and was beginning to cry. I'd never seen him do this.

It was hard news.

My dad survived the crash but was paralyzed from the waist down. My brother and I didn't talk about how we felt with each other or with anyone who asked. Julia was withdrawn and simply cried and cried. We just tried to comfort and protect her.

How could another bad thing like this happen to me?

✳

My dad was able to work from home from then on, but he suffered from other side effects from the accident, and his health just never bounced back to the way that it was. He seemed weaker and weaker inside and out to me and, at age 15, again, I didn't like to see this.

He made great efforts to be a good father and especially put energy into connecting with me. He came to all of my games and would even sit and quietly watch some of my practices, encouraging me afterwards. It felt good, I should say, but I was always a little mad inside. I wished my dad could've been able to play with me. I wished that he could wrestle and shoot hoops. I wished that he could've made Mom stay.

✳

The first time I learned to drive, he told me step by step what to do. It was his new Land Cruiser, custom made to accommodate his disability. We were in the driveway, getting ready to take a trial run in the neighborhood. I nervously turned the key in the ignition. Without thinking, I put my foot down on the accelerator, while shifting the car into reverse, and apparently my foot was a bit more adept than my hand, because the car loudly revved, the gear landed in drive, and we went crashing into our garage door.

Out of the corner of my eye, I could see my dad's head nearly hit the dashboard as I slammed on the breaks. At the same time, his arm shot out in front of my chest, instinctively trying to hold me back. We stopped and both were staring straight ahead. What he was going to say or do next, I had no idea. Ben and Julia came running out of the house, mouths gaping open. Julia's hands went to her head, as I read her lips, "*Oh Jacob!*"

I then heard something totally out of context. It was laughter. I turned to see my dad still looking straight ahead, laughing, as if he just had heard the greatest joke and punch line ever. I exhaled but was not sure that I saw the humor.

I cautiously began to laugh, joining him, thankful that he wasn't swearing at me. Ben and Julia watched him through the windshield, perplexed. He began to howl and shake. For some reason, my laughter became genuine, as I took in the irony of the whole situation. We laughed so hard, we cried. We couldn't get words out, as we reenacted the crash. He used his sleeves to wipe the tears off his cheeks. Ben and Julia gave up on us, shook their heads, and went inside.

※

The next spring, I injured my knee during one of my games, and my world fell apart for the rest of the season . . . my routine of school, baseball, and friends collapsed. My pain, both inside and out, started emerging through the void. Without baseball, I felt lost. It felt unbearable.

During that time, one of my friends took me to a party, and there was some marijuana being passed around. My friends were there laughing and having fun. A girl from my chemistry class, Lisa, passed it to me and smiled with eyebrows raised in an offer. The freedom and fun that I felt in that room was new to me, and aside from the strange smell and earlier warnings in my life against drugs, I was willing to give it a try. I wanted to escape my pain badly, and it worked.

I came to my next big decision then. I decided that pain was the problem and that I would keep it as far away from me as I possibly could, whatever it took. I would not be the kind of person who gets hurt over and over again.

✳

The next year, my brother went off to college, and his absence wasn't even felt for the most part. The only thing that I noticed was that my dad now had more time to be aware of my sister and me. I didn't like this because he began to notice that I was sometimes fine and sometimes "out of it," as he described it. For months, I was under the radar, but now all of the sudden he was acting overly concerned. We had many uncomfortable talks that year about the effects of drugs and setting boundaries. It made me mad.

I wanted to have fun. *Maybe Mom left him because he was boring.*

It was a typical high school scene: friends would come over when my dad left, we'd light up on the back porch where there was plenty of fresh air to hide the smell, we'd laugh, be stupid, maybe pass out, and my dad would have me clean up the next day and usually put me on restriction again.

One day, a friend and I ended up in a tattoo shop after one of these afternoons, and I was the first to put my arm up on the counter. I pulled a torn piece of paper from a magazine, folded in my pocket and opened it for the heavily pierced, redheaded artist to see. "Right here," I said. "I want this."

"Gandhi?" she asked.

"Dude, not Gandhi. What's wrong with you?" asked my friend, Zach, who already had about four tattoos, all on the theme of rock music.

"No, not the picture. The words that I wrote below the picture, that's what I want." I said.

A few weeks earlier, I was eating lunch in the kitchen at home, and I noticed one of my dad's magazines opened on the table, to an article about India. I flipped through it, only really interested in the pictures. A page or two into the article, there was a photo of Gandhi, looking nearly dead, being held in the arms of someone the photographer didn't allow to be seen. His face was severely withdrawn. The caption read, "Although Gandhi endured pain and suffering, as seen here at the peak of his fast, his solitary determination to sacrifice the pleasures of his life for the sake of the cause, was unlike that of any others' of his time."

I was disturbed and captivated. *Pain . . . suffering . . . solitary . . . sacrificing the pleasures of his life . . .* I stared at the photo for several minutes, really studying this picture of a weak, sad, and lonely looking life, and realized that this was something I never wanted to be. The clarity of this thought and the distaste I felt were so strong that I tore the photo off the page, stuck it in my pocket, left my lunch unfinished, and walked away.

I pinned that photo to my bulletin board in my room and looked at it often over the next several days. Something about it held my attention with unusual interest. *What is it?*

One night, I took out a pad of paper and began messing around with words as I glanced at the photo. Then, I landed on it. This is where Gandhi and I met, only for opposite reasons. Two things I wanted to keep out of my life no matter what: Suffering and being alone.

"What does it say behind the barbed wire?" asked the girl behind the counter as she stared at it.

"'Suffering'. And I want that repeated around my bicep, with the wire running over it," I explained. "Can you do it so that you can read the words under the wire?"

"Wow . . . That's heavy," said Zach.

"Yeah, I think I can," said the girl, "I'll make the lettering a different color and a thicker font, and the wiring thin over it."

And, in the end, I held and squeezed a tennis ball as she needled the words into my skin.

✳

As the end of high school approached, decisions about college and what next began to press in. I had two separate lives going in full force by this time: at home, I was quiet, tried to be kind to Julia, and civil to my dad. I tried to do the things they asked, so they wouldn't bother me. Away from home, I was a different person. I had turned 18 that fall and was signing my own excuses out of class and barely passing. I was with friends, partying, or with one girlfriend or another, disappearing in some bedroom, or car, or wherever. I couldn't wait to get away from home and let all of the expectations go and live the life that I wanted.

When my dad was in that accident, he received quite a bit of money as a result. Much of it went to his medical bills, but there was still a large amount that he put into an account for each of us children, hoping that it would send us through college and pay for a house someday.

Well, I knew this. But I didn't want anything to do with future plans. I wanted it all now, to decide on my own what to do with it. I decided after the holidays, my senior year, I would ask my dad for it.

※

It was New Year's Day. I was lying around, watching football, hung-over from the night before. My head was pounding, the taste in my mouth was sour, and I couldn't seem to quench my thirst. But by late afternoon, after a steady stream of Tylenol, I gathered my courage to ask him.

He was sitting in his wheel chair, next to the couch. He was cheering for the under-dog, which was typical, and was watching a new Budweiser commercial made especially for the bowl games. He loved watching these games and had snacks and drinks surrounding him as if he were snowed in from a winter storm. He laughed at its ending and threw down a handful of honey roasted peanuts.

"Dad, I need to ask you something."

He looked up a little startled, with a slight smile, and raised eyebrows. I couldn't remember the last time I'd begun a conversation with him, and I winced a bit that his expression seemed perhaps, hopeful, and eager in some way. He obviously had no idea what I was about to ask. I'm sure that this thought had never entered his mind.

I cleared my throat. "Well, Dad, I've been thinking a lot. I've been thinking about college and my future. And . . . I don't think it's for me, Dad."

Pause. Silence.

"What do you mean, son?"

"I can't do it, Dad."

"What can't you do?"

I sat up on the couch and put my head into my hands. I took a deep breath. The game was back on, and I heard my dad pick up the remote control and mute the sound.

Julia was singing along with Joni Mitchell on the radio in her room: " . . . they paved paradise, and put up a parking lot." Somehow, her sweet voice and the happy nature of the tune were sickening to me. I forced myself back to my dad.

"I can't be like everyone else, or Ben, and go to college

and continue being a student. I'm different, and I want to go away. I want to travel, and I want to do whatever I feel like doing." The momentum of my craving propelled me on. "And this is a hard thing to ask for, Dad, but I want the money you've set aside for me, for my future . . . only, I want it now."

I couldn't read the expression on his face yet. It reminded me of watching some political dignitary on CSPAN when they're in an international meeting, and they have an earpiece in, awaiting the interpreter's translation.

"Dad, I want you to trust me and let me make my own decisions with the money that's mine."

Even as I said it, I didn't believe it myself. I didn't believe I was trustworthy, and I couldn't believe I was calling that money "mine."

After several moments in silence, he slowly picked up the remote again and turned the sound back on, saying nothing. His head slowly fell back against the cushion behind him, and he was biting his lower lip. He had his head turned back to the television, but he was somewhere else, not responding to the game at all. Just as I got up to leave the room, I noticed a tear drop down his cheek.

Oh great . . . now I've made him cry again.

✳

We had many conversations about this over the next few months, but when it was all said and done, my dad gave in and said yes. Who knows, maybe he was tired of our growing distance, too, and in the end he said to me, "Jacob, this isn't about the money. I can see that you're determined to go and pull away right now." I couldn't tell if this meant yes, or no, and I waited.

The swing was creaking as I pushed off the post of the back porch with my foot and stared at the oak tree I'd known all my life. The old tree house still stood perched in its center, covered in faded green and brown paint now, with its remaining original sign, "Keep out!"

"Jacob, I am going to give you the money. I am going to trust you to become who you want to become. And, I'm going to trust you to remember where you've come from and that you are loved here." His eyes were full of tears, and his large, warm hand landed on my shoulder, as the swing stopped.

Although I wanted to look away, he seemed determined to hold my gaze. I literally pushed against him and shrugged away from his touch. It was too much for me.

"Thanks. Thanks so much, Dad." And that was it. I had my money.

✳

Things went fast from then on. By spring break, I was gone, literally, and thus ended my "high school career." I didn't have the courage to tell Dad and Julia, face-to-face, that I was leaving. I didn't tell school, or for that matter any of my friends. I just drove away one morning.

The house had been quiet the night before. I threw a few changes of clothes into a bag, and brought Charlie and Emma, our two yellow labs, into my room to sleep with me. They were used to sleeping with Julia and eventually left my room for their familiar place for the night. I wrote a short note, saying that I had to go, but that I would be in touch, and that I would be fine.

After a sleepless couple of hours, I walked through the house in the dark to the kitchen, and left the note on the table, under a glass saltshaker. I walked out the door, bag in hand, and I left.

✳

Over the next two or three years, Ben, who I hadn't heard from but once or twice over the time he was away at school, tried repeatedly to reach me by phone, email, and text message. I never answered, until one time long after I was away when he must have called from a friend's phone. I didn't recognize the number. I thought maybe it was a girl who I had been with recently.

"Jacob! What the hell are you doing?" he asked.

"Ben! Hey how's it going?" I passively replied.

"Jacob, you are seriously throwing your life away, and Dad's money as well. What are you doing, Jacob?" his voice was livid with anger. The words coming through his clenched teeth were nearly visible to me.

"Ben, you don't understand. I'm fine. Dad's money, which is mine by the way, is being well used. You take things too seriously," I said coolly, attempting to calm him down. As I replied, though, I felt the buzz of my nightly "high" still ringing in my head and told myself to be careful while I talked.

I rolled over in the cheap hotel bed and woke my partner. We had found each other at the bar on the corner the night before. The room was strewn with cigarettes and bottles, and the TV was still on. I stood up, walked to the window, and cracked it open for some fresh air. Below, a sign read "Piedmont Avenue," the street sweeping machine was doing its morning run, and the newsstand was just opening. The man tending the stand wore a black beanie with grey hair coming out around the edges and a scowl on his face while he hurriedly tried to stack the day's papers.

"Jacob, what's wrong with you? Are you high? Where are you now?" Ben's voice switched in tone a little, and I couldn't read it.

"I don't know, man. I mean I'm in Atlanta, but I don't know this city well." I stalled. *Why did he want to know where I was?*

A beautiful woman in a red flowered dress with long legs walked up to get a paper from the man. She tilted her head as she spoke with him and began to laugh. His expression softened. He found her paper for her, they exchanged the paper for money, and she walked away. As he watched her, his eyes wandered, and he began smiling unbeknownst to him.

"Jacob, I want to see you," Ben said haltingly.

"What?" *He's got to be kidding.* "Ben, you haven't wanted to see me in ... well ... I don't think you ever *have* wanted to see me. No, Ben. I'm doing this on my own. I'm fine and everything is good." Click.

That was it. I got dressed, gathered my things, and left my phone there. I didn't ever want another call.

✳

I decided to get further away and disappear. I left no traces for my family, or anyone, to find me. For the next several years, I traveled with my money and spent most of my time down somewhere in South America. Brazil seemed to be the most enticing. The drugs were easy to find, women and sex were readily available, even if I did have to pay sometimes, and the culture was full of pleasure and parties.

There was a woman in particular whom I couldn't resist. Her name was Sandra, and we ended up together often. Her family had money as well, so we kept it simple, had a lot of fun, and spent each day spontaneously doing whatever we wanted to do.

Sandra seemed to really understand me, and yet, she had no expectations. When she listened to me talk, sometimes I would have a flashback of my mother, often of the times we would sit on the porch together, and then I would push that away as quickly as possible.

Early on, she noticed my tattoo. "What's that about?" she asked as we lay on the beach that day.

I told her, in the briefest of words, then took a sip of my drink.

She looked up at a kite flying high above us. "Well, it seems you know whom you don't want to be like," she smiled and turned to me. "Do you have another one that tells who you *do* want to be like?"

"It's the same thing, Sandra, who I'm not and who I am . . . all the same. What's the matter, don't you like who I am?" She was either satisfied or lost interest because we watched the kite for a bit longer, got up and took a swim, and never talked about it again.

I never contacted my family. In fact, I had not had one conversation with my dad since I left. I wondered about Julia a few times, wondered what she looked like and what she was doing with her life. But, thoughts of home were always brief.

✳

One evening, I pulled up to a hotel I was going to stay in for the night and had the valet park my car. I gave the desk my card to run for the room, and they said that it was "denied." *Couldn't be.* I gave them a different card, and it too, came back denied.

"Sir, I'm sorry, would you like to pay in another form tonight?" said the clerk.

All motion suddenly stopped. I noticed everything around me, as if the frame of a photo had captured the stillness. The clerk's hair was meticulously styled, and his uniform was flawlessly pressed. The elevator light was on floor 12, and the couple standing in front of it, waiting for a ride, were arm in arm, perhaps 40 or 50 years old, and looked like they'd just come in from a late dinner.

Is this it? The moment the money is gone? I wiped the back of my hand against my lip to find beads of sweat forming.

I feigned a look of surprise and frustration, and said I would look into that then quickly excused myself. I got in my car, drove to a nearby park, and slept there for the night. In the morning, after my quick fix of getting high, I figured it was time to get a job. I was living in Buzios, a town on the coast of Brazil, where I had been for the last eight months or so.

I was turned away everywhere I went. The economy in Brazil had been declining for a while now, and jobs were becoming more and more difficult to find. In addition, and more common for me, were the many excuses given and the looks of disapproval and repulsion I received over and over.

The final rejection was from a man at a shoe-shining stand in a hotel. "I'm sorry, but I can hardly pay the two boys I have working for me now," were his words.

When I told Sandra about it later, she said, "Jacob, no

one will hire you, you're a waste, don't you know that? You've burned everyone here. Everyone." Her disgust was glaring. "You don't have an address, you don't have references for a job, and you're high all the time. What did you think would happen when you ran out of money?"

Sandra was gone in the morning. I never saw her again. When the money ran out, so did she.

I began to sell anything I owned, or trade them for meals. I had a few bags of clothes in my car, and that helped me get through a few days. The stereo in my car was removable, and that fed me for a while longer. I continued sleeping in my car, finding hidden places to park and sleep. As time went on with no job or plan to turn my circumstances around, I began to fear having to sell the only two things I had left that were valuable to me.

The car was obvious. It was a classic corvette that I had had shipped from the states. I'd received so much attention from its silvery blue shine that people in the small village always knew me, where I was, and when I arrived. This was a problem now that I was out of money. I couldn't hide. But, at least I knew the car was worth something, and if I had to, I could sell it, and hopefully get out of this hole.

The other thing of value I owned was a ring.

※

A year after my mother had left, my dad went through

this phase where he wanted to "bring us together as a family."

He was barbecuing steaks and vegetables on the grill when I got home from baseball practice that evening. The table was set on our back porch, with a few bottles of sparkling cider in the middle. *Why is he doing this? What bad news does he have to give us now?* Ben and Julia sat waiting at the table, quietly watching him with wide eyes.

When I returned from washing my hands inside, they were all seated waiting for me. I sat down next to him and noticed that we all had a small box on our plate, even my dad.

"What's this?" I asked.

"I . . ." he cleared his throat, "I have something for each of us."

"Why did you wrap it for yourself if it's from you?" Julia said openly with a smile. My dad's smile surfaced at this, and he continued.

"I've been thinking about something for awhile now. We don't talk about it much, but since your mom left, I think we've had a hard time."

"It's not her fault," I said before I could stop myself.

The pained look on his face told me instantly that I shouldn't have said that.

He continued, "I didn't mean that, Jacob. I'm just saying that we've had a hard time for a while now. I want to give you each something that tells you we are still a family, that we are connected, and we're going to make it." He paused and picked up the box on his plate. "Will you each open your box?"

Even though a 13-year-old boy and not into jewelry, I was intrigued by the ring in front of me. It was a gold band with a black, flat square onyx stone in the center of it. In the middle of the stone, was a small and beautiful diamond. As I looked up, I saw that we each had the same ring.

My dad slipped his ring onto his right hand, middle finger. "This, to me, and I hope it will be to each of you, is a symbol that we can all share together and draw strength from. Like I said, I know that we are facing some tough things, but I want us to know that we're not alone."

"Thanks, Dad," Ben said quickly. "It's really nice. This is nice of you."

"I love it!" said Julia, as she popped up from her chair and threw her arms around his neck from behind. His hands covered her little arms and patted them softly, as he looked over at me.

Although I thought it all a bit corny and dramatic, I couldn't bring myself to convey this and ended up saying, "Thanks, Dad. That's cool."

That night, as I looked it over before falling asleep in bed, I noticed I could see my reflection in the gold metal. My face looked oblong and fat, as if looking in a mirror at a carnival fun house. Then I noticed some words inscribed on the inside of the ring that said, "*You belong.*"

Why didn't he say anything about this at the table? Do all of the rings say this? Or just mine? Over the next several days, one by one, I was able to somehow confirm that these words were inscribed on each of our rings.

✳

And so, this was the ring that I now stared at, wondering how much money I could get for it at one of the local boutiques. I had no idea of its worth. I pulled up to the most popular shop on the village square and walked in. The woman working there was minimally nice to me. She wore her velvet black hair up on the top of her head. The deep creases in her skin spoke of sun exposure and years of worry. She asked how she could help.

I took the ring off my finger and set it on the counter. She raised her eyebrows as she looked at it, and then up at me. "Are you wanting to sell this?"

"Yes," I said, as I nodded.

"It's pretty scratched up, but the stone and the diamond are of value and retrievable" she assessed.

"What do you think you can give me for it?" I carefully asked.

"Probably seventy five or so," she trailed off, as she held it up to the light and reached for a magnifying glass to look closely at the stones. "I don't think you'll find any place that will give you more than that for a weathered setting like this. There will be some work to restore it."

"Seventy five hundred?"

"No, dollars," she said flatly, squarely looking me

in the eye.

"I'll take it." I desperately said, forgetting my earlier
notions of bartering. No sooner had I said this to her, than I
heard tires squealing outside the boutique. I thought I would
hear the crash of cars colliding but didn't. I instinctively
reached for my car keys in my pocket and found it empty.

I turned and ran out of the shop to see the final seconds
of my car disappearing around the corner and out of sight. I
ran to the corner and tried to see a trace of where it went, but
nothing. I could still hear it squealing blocks away, and I saw a
policeman get in his car and speed off to chase it; however,
time would tell that no one could catch the thief who stole my
car.

The seventy-five dollars from the ring was gone in a
day, after a meal and a night's worth of drowning my sorrows.
My last "Hurrah!" is what I told myself . . . and it was.

There was one "soup kitchen" on the outskirts of the
village, but I was too proud to get food there. Then, I
remembered this guy, whose name I couldn't recall, who I
partied with a while back, whose father had a small farm
outside of town. After a night's sleep on a park bench under a
blanket of newspapers and a few saltine crackers I had stolen
from the village coffee shop, I took the next day and walked
out to the farm. I felt horrible as I walked. I had run out of
the stash of marijuana I always kept, my head was pounding,
and I had chills.

My party friend's dad was onto me the minute he saw

me. I was filthy, looked like a skinny druggy, and was a mess. He told me I could try his neighbor three miles away who had a "*sitio de porco*," small pig farm. I was hungry, desperate, and had no other plan, so I set foot again for the next stop.

I arrived just after sunset that evening, and the neighbor wasn't too excited to see me either. He was eating dinner with his family. I could smell the meal, and my stomach was cramping and turning with hunger. I couldn't keep my eyes from tearing, as my situation became more and more desperate. His wife was in the background, wiping her hands on her apron. She didn't smile and turned away as I was telling my story. Children were laughing somewhere in the house. *And that smell, Oh God, what is that amazing smell?*

The neighbor told me that he couldn't promise anything, but for tonight I could stay out in the barn with the pigs, handed me a blanket, and slammed the door. "*Obrigada,*" I whispered in Portuguese thanks, as I stood alone, grasping the blanket, outside of his house.

It was getting cold by now, and the pigs were settling in together, in their muddied stalls. They were disgusting, and they stunk. I was hungry, so very hungry. I saw a bucket of pig slop about five feet away from where I was trying to clear an area to lay for the night.

I looked around, and no one was in site, just the pigs and me. They were snorting and burrowing in for their night's sleep. The smell took me back to the dirty animal stalls at the San Francisco Zoo during feeding time. I'd been on numerous field trips during elementary school.

The silver bucket of feed was rusted, and the handle was broken. The clod of mud sitting on the top spoke to the congealed slop that was holding it up.

My stomach growled, as I looked around again for any sign of people nearby. No one.

So, I did it.

I reached in the bucket, scooped out the mud clod, and pulled up a handful of grainy slop, with chunks of what looked like corn, and what else, I didn't want to know. I had to pull out a few pieces of hay that had fallen in the bucket. I closed my eyes and swallowed quickly. It was salty, gritty, and horrible tasting, but would have to work. I strained from gagging and gulped down about four or five more handfuls before running as far as I could get from my blanket and throwing it all up.

I fell over on my damp blanket and stared up at the sky. My eyes were stinging.

What's going to happen to me? How am I going to get out of this? Sandra was right . . . No one wants to help me. I just couldn't believe that in a matter of days, I was this bad off. Or was it more like months, or maybe even years . . . I didn't want to figure that out right now. I was panicked about the next meal, and for that matter, about everything.

"Jacob, I am going to give you the money. I am going to trust you to become who you want to become."

I hadn't thought of these words in so long.

"I am going to trust you to become who you want to become," my dad had said.

What was he thinking? Why did he do this to me? I did become who I wanted to become. And I hated it. I didn't only hate that I was with pigs and eating their food and homeless. What I hated more was how I felt about everything, about Sandra and many other women and seeming "friends" along the way.

This ball of hate snowballed and grew larger and larger. I hated the pain I still felt about my mom, and I hated my thoughts I'd always had about my dad.

I hate myself. I am a waste.

My fingers were combing through my hair. My forehead was wet with perspiration. With growing anxiety, my hands moved more rapidly. I began gripping my hair, and pulling hard, until I realized, without thinking I'd ripped out a handful. I stared at the strands of my hair in my closed fist as if they were from someone else, surreally detached. My blanket cinched up around my body as I curled my knees into my chest. Closing my eyes as tight as I could, I began to see images and shapes, as if looking through a kaleidoscope, and a wave of downward spiraling emotion washed over me. I thought I was passing out.

Just then, I heard an odd sound come from somewhere within me, a sound I couldn't suppress. It was a moan, no . . . a groan, coming to the surface. I recognized the feeling: regret. Yes, regret. Years of self-absorption began bubbling up as if toxic waste, burning through my chest. And then, sobs, uncontrollable sobs.

Why? Why had I been so stupid? Why was love, and everything in my life so ugly and painful? I couldn't stop crying. Every thought rousted more pain, more memory, and more ache.

When my tears ran dry, I was fatigued from the emptying. My last thought as I fell asleep, was . . . *I would die if he saw me like this.*

✳

The sunlight woke me the next morning. Moments after, I heard the neighbor walk up and tell me that I had to leave by noon, but that if I wanted a meal, I would need to clean the stalls and feed the pigs this morning.

I stood up and felt dizzy. I was in a daze. I couldn't remember all that I had thought about the night before, but I remembered crying like I'd never done before. The neighbor's offer, although there was nothing warm about it, made sense. *Of course, I'd work for a meal.*

As I slowly began raking the hay and mud away from the walls and began hosing it down, I considered the slop that I ate and threw up the night before. I had a memory unexpectedly pop up of Julia feeding Charlie and Emma years ago. I smiled. My breath was suddenly shallow. A wave of panic washed over me. A surprising longing for this moment of warmth from home hadn't happened in years.

I was lost staring at the slop, standing totally still. And it occurred to me, the irony of the situation. *Here I was, destitute, somewhere in Brazil, eating pig slop, while I could be eating, at least, with Charlie and Emma at home.* Another smile. Another deep ache.

How did I get so messed up? Even though I don't deserve anything from anyone in my family, especially my dad, wouldn't it be better to be there, and maybe gardening and working somehow for my dad, rather than here, or wherever, eating this?

When I left years ago, my family had already received a lot of attention in our community. First with my mom leaving us and then with my dad's accident, we had become the town's "poster child," so to speak. We were given everything from "meals-on-wheels," to organized rides to school and practices for us kids, even a community scholarship fund, more from goodwill and sympathy than need, where people gave money to help me, Ben, and Julia make it to college.

What must all of those people have thought, when I took the family money, took their money, and ran away, before even finishing high school? And to think of Ben and Julia dealing with this and becoming the "face" to the town of the ungrateful son, the disappointing failure. I wondered, sadly, for the first time, if I had perhaps ruined the communities' well intent toward our family altogether.

I tried to imagine returning.

Maybe my dad would yell, unload on me, and send me away. I could see that. Or maybe he would force me to clean up and make-

up for all that I've lost, before I could ever be considered part of the family again ... I could see that as well.

Still, the thought of earning my way back, whatever I'd have to do and for however long I'd have to do it, seemed a better option than where I was now. *This ... was nothing. This ... offers nothing.*

The next decision of my life, then, became clear: I was going to do everything possible, within my power, whatever was left, to make my way home. *Home.* It was as real as anything to me now. I would fight to get home and beg for a job from my dad or earn my way through a treatment program, whatever it took. I would sign anything and agree to anything.

✳

After lunch, I took the whole day and walked back to the village. It was hot once again, probably in the nineties, and the heat felt like a heavy blanket pressing around me. A few cars and farm trucks passed on the road, but instead of attempting to hitch a ride, I walked with what felt like necessary steps. I didn't know why, but each bead of sweat that dripped off my nose and chin seemed to splash and echo. The waves of the heat on the road made me feel delusional. For all I know, I was. My mouth began to crack in the corners from the dryness. *Step, step, step ... keep going ... go home.*

Somehow the pain felt right. The dryness, the without-ness of it all, was what I deserved. I started to crave the pain in each stride. I felt a blister forming on the outside of my right heal, and like a mosquito bite begging for attention, I began to land all of my weight, with each step, on that spot. Eventually, I saw blood soaking through my shoe, and that felt right.

As I entered the village that night, I went straight to the train station, walking as if mildly intoxicated and spoke with the ticket agent. My head was swimming with exhaustion, but my heart was so focused that nothing seemed to tempt distraction.

"I need to get home. I know you know me, and that I haven't been respectable in any way. But, I need a break, and I need to go home."

"Jacob, you're a mess." The shock on her face sobered me to my appearance. "Why is today different than any other day? You've been an asshole ever since you came to town last year," she said. My heart sank. Her name was Elise, and I'd known her over the months, and I think I spent a few nights at her place. Her eyes were cold with loathing, her smile was bitter, and she seemed to enjoy the power she wielded over me now.

"Yes. Yes, you're right, Elise. You have no reason to help me now. But, I need to go home. Will you please help me, if for no other reason, than to get rid of me?" I pleaded. My head hung low, and I could no longer look her in the eye, anticipating her refusal.

I started to panic on the inside. My road back home

was in her hands. I had no charm left to offer, no power to buy my way through the anger of her heart. *"Please,"* I called out silently in my mind. *"Please."* She lit herself a cigarette and drew on it slowly. "Please, help me," it slipped out aloud. Another slow drag and exhale of smoke.

"Jacob, you son-of-a-bitch! You are so manipulative. You're right, I can get rid of you and rid our town of the likes of you for good." She began printing something out and stamping it two or three times with all of the anger she had been holding against me. Then she shoved the tickets through the hole in the glass window. *"Saia d'aquí, Jacó! E não volte nunca mais!"* . . . "Get out of here Jacob! Don't ever come back!"

In my hands were train tickets to Rio de Janeiro. Relief and disgust hit me all at once. *What a fool I've been.* But, I took the tickets and caught the next train out of town.

Getting the plane flight was a similar scenario. I begged for some money on the street to afford a call to Sandra, whose uncle was a travel agent in the village. She nearly hung up on me but ended up listening to my desperate request for help. She, too, gave me the same parting speech of never wanting to see or hear from me again but luckily, persuaded her uncle to arrange for the flight home.

※

As I found my seat in aisle 24, I sat down with no bags and empty hands. People were staring at me. The two people who were seated next to me left and took vacant seats elsewhere once the plane was fully boarded. I avoided eye contact and sank low in my seat. I was still wearing the same clothes that I had on when I stayed at the farm. I smelled like manure and sweat. I was so tired. I was tired of the recent days, but more, I was tired of the years I'd lived. I felt like I was 20 years older than I really was. So tired. So empty.

I wonder if he'll even recognize me again . . . I thought as I fell asleep.

✳

I woke with a start. The pilot was announcing our descent into San Francisco. My heart raced. I sat up and suddenly felt a little sick. *What am I doing? There is no way he'll take me back.* I asked the man across the isle if he had a pen, found a few napkins, and began writing some words I could use to explain to my father. I was painfully nervous.

The familiar resound of shame was overwhelming me. *I'm nothing. I don't matter to anyone. I've screwed up too much this time.*

What other choices do I have? "Father, please help me." I scribbled that out. "Dad, why did you give me that money?" Scratch that. "Dad, forgive me." *Yes.* "I no longer deserve to be called your son." *Yes.*

I read the napkin over and over. I worked on memorizing the lines of my script, eyes closed, imagining the street and the driveway. Our house was set on an angle, so you could enter to the front side, or you could walk around to the left where the back yard opened to a beautiful little meadow with a stream that ran most of the year down below. There were old trees all around it, and I wondered if the swing set was still there. Before I knew it, a few tears fell from my eyes. The longing was palpable. I thought I heard myself faintly moan again.

✳

The plane arrived at San Francisco International Airport at 3:30 am. I walked out to the curb outside of baggage claim, and it became clear that no one was lingering around, or interested in helping a homeless guy at this time of night. No bus or shuttle driver would stop to talk to me. I could have tried to find a spot to sleep up against the terminal but could already see the security guard eyeing me, ready to ask me to leave. Getting through customs had been rough enough, and I was eager to leave the place.

There was a woman in her 60s or 70s from the plane, who ended up near me on the outside curb. I had passed her a time or two while boarding and leaving the plane, and each time she smiled kindly at me. My discouragement must have shown all over my face because when I looked over to her on the curb, her face looked at me with sympathy.

"Is someone coming for you?" she asked.

"No, I think I'm on my own." I stalled, not sure if I

should be bothering an old woman for help. "I'll figure something out, though. How about you? Will your ride be here soon?" I probed.

"Yes," she said, "my son will be here soon to give me a ride. I live over in the Marina District. Is that anywhere near where you need to go?" Again, she gently smiled at me.

"It's closer than I am now." I conceded, breathing a sigh of relief.

Her name was Claire, and she was returning from a trip to see her sister. She had lived in the city her whole life and had retired eight years ago from San Francisco Unified School District. She had taught high school English for 37 years. Most people I had known over the years who had been teaching long were cynical and tired. She was neither. She talked about teaching as though it was the joy of her life. Her kindness warmed me.

Her son pulled up to the curb in an older white van with writing on it. As he came around the front to meet her, my eyes quickly noticed his collar and then the cigarette hanging from his mouth. "Mission District's Van of Mercy" it said on the side, in black and gold large block print. *This is going to be interesting.* He looked me over a few times, probably thinking the same thing.

Claire introduced me to her son, Carl, who was a priest. He greeted me warmly, and shook my hand. No hesitation. We got Claire settled in the front seat, and I hopped in the back. They talked over the flight, and how her visit with her sister had gone, while he puffed on his cigarette and smiled warmly and lovingly at his mother. The ache of my heart went into my throat so unannounced that I coughed to gain control.

"So, Jacob, it looks like you're going home?" Carl asked as we got onto the freeway. *How did he know that?*

"Uh, yeah, I guess you could say that." I grew quiet.

Claire broke in, "I hope it goes well for you, Jacob." My eyes immediately began to sting.

"Yeah, me too, Claire." I was able to get out in a whisper.

We arrived at Claire's apartment, at the end of Scott Street, still long before daybreak. From her place, you could see the Golden Gate Bridge. Carl offered me a place to stay at the church, but I thanked him and set out on foot from there. I couldn't wait, or pause, any longer. I decided that I would just keep moving toward home, by foot, or by car, or bus, or whatever it took.

※

As I came to the bridge after a miserable walk through the cold, damp fog, the ocean wind was freezing and felt like it was blowing right through me. Maybe it was.

"You look like you need a drink."

Just before the tollbooth and off against the bayside railings, sat a man huddled next to a trashcan. He had on a grey beanie, a dark green jacket, faded black jeans, and work boots with no socks. He smiled underneath a beard of salt and pepper hair, straggling over his lips. His eyes were on me, but they had that familiar gloss of gratified numbness.

My mouth watered. *A drink. Sounds so good. Yes, that would calm my nerves, and would warm me up.* I took a few steps toward him. *Thank God! This is what I need before I go home. I can't go back in the shape I'm in!*

He grabbed a brown sack tucked against his chest inside his jacket and held it out towards me. "Here you go buddy, you won't be sorry. This shit clears the mind and warms the soul." He broke out into a cackling sort of laugh that made me pause a moment. He was missing two teeth. He looked completely content.

I could taste it in my mouth before the bottle ever hit my lips. It rolled down my throat familiarly, as if I'd slipped on my favorite, most comfortable, old sweatshirt that I never ended up giving away. I took a deep breath and felt the warmth through my body. The instant rush to my head was relieving. *I'm going to be fine now.*

As I tipped the bottle for another drink, his hand reached out and swiped the bag back. He shouted, "That's enough! You think this stuff grows on trees?" It was abrupt. His expression turned hostile.

I had a fleeting desire to reach over and tear the bag out of his hands and run with it, but I thought otherwise as I caught a glimpse of the guard on duty regarding us from the bridge.

I watched as my not-so-long-ago, drunken reflection, stuffed the bottle back into his jacket, stumbled away from me, and then turned and left the lit area of the bridge and disappeared. I would have been willing to join him, however, I wasn't invited.

Alone again, I turned and faced the bridge, took a deep breath, and was back to my mantra: *step, step, step . . . keep going . . . go home.*

I felt a little euphoric, as many people do as they approach the old, magnificent red arches. It was dark out still, and even though this bridge and the Bay Area were familiar to me from long ago, I was never there as the person I'd become, and the feelings were totally different now.

As I began to walk out over the water, I looked at the edge of the bridge. I turned and stopped and stared at the railing as my breath became shallow. I walked over to the edge and looked down into the cold, dark lapping depth. The white caps on the water appeared and faded rhythmically, luring me into deep thought.

Is this it? Maybe this would be best. I wouldn't have to face him. Maybe they'd all end up feeling sorry for me in the end. I began to think about this. The guard was now about 50 yards back and keeping his eye on me.

I yearned for this cold ocean wind to really reach me, on the inside. I wanted it to literally blow through me, to touch every dark and hurting area of my body. I suddenly began to unbutton my shirt. I took it off and stood on it.

Next I took off my pants, my shoes, and then my socks and stood on them. I stood in front of the rail, in my boxers, freezing, and wondered: *What next?* My arms began to lift and spread out, side to side, and I began to cry. "Blow through me," I whispered, "blow through me now." Tears again, began to fall, hot against my cheeks. "Reach me. Blow through me. Take it all away."

As cold as I felt on the outside, the sensation on the inside was warming me. Several moments passed. I don't know what was happening to me. I was nearly passed out when I heard the guard, "Okay, buddy, time to move on." I quickly brought in my arms and lowered my head. He was pacing about ten yards away now, "Let's go buddy. Put your clothes back on. You'll freeze out here," he condescendingly said.

I dressed quickly and clumsily kicked one of my shoes off the edge of the bridge. My sock was getting a hole in the heel. *I've got to keep moving,* I told myself. I continued crossing over the bridge again, now with a bit of an uneven gate. I tried to breathe deeply, and focus on the lights of Sausalito ahead. The change in the light of dawn was beginning now, and soon I would see the hills and surroundings of my past.

On the far side of the bridge, there was a little bus stop bench, sheltered in a clear plexiglass frame. I sat down hard and wondered how I would make it home from here. It was probably only another 10 to 15 miles but to walk that, in my shape, well, I wondered if I could do it. I decided to rest a moment before going on and stretched out on the bench.

What had just happened to me out there on the bridge?

I watched the fog rolling into the bay through the glass covering above me. *How would I ever be able to describe that? Maybe I wouldn't ever want to.* My eyelids grew heavy and exhaustion took over.

✳

The sound of an incoming bus jolted me awake. I jumped, then, remembered where I was. The sun was shining overhead, and the mid-day temperature was up to the 60s, I guessed. I must've fallen into a deep sleep because the bay traffic looked as though it was well into its daily routine. The driver pulled up to the bus stop and opened the door. "Are you boarding?" asked the grey haired, heavy-set white man, with no smile, as he kept his eyes ahead through the front windshield.

"I'd like to," was all I could say.

"Then, let's go," he said abruptly.

I took the risk and stood up quickly, then got on. Something about the way he said that seemed to have whisked me into prompt action without much thinking. I walked past the coin stand for tickets and sat right behind the driver. I sat very still, wondering what would happen next. I tried to be invisible, as if one could do such a thing, and hoped that he

wouldn't ask for money. I waited and remained still as he
drove off.

"What stop?" he asked.

"Tiburon Boulevard," I quickly replied, matching his
tempo.

With no glance back, or any words, he reached out to
the meter and dropped in ten quarters. As I got off at my stop,
I quietly thanked him, and as he closed the door, I heard him
say, "Good luck."

I was now in my hometown, and a fresh wave of nerves
began to surround me. I felt like I didn't belong here
anymore. I needed to keep practicing my lines, and my nerves
made me feel like I had injected straight shots of espresso into
my veins.

I walked past the shopping area, noticing new
restaurants and cafes where people were sitting out enjoying a
leisurely late lunch. I began walking along the street and into
the hills, toward Mount Tam.

The first really familiar place I passed was the library.
After a few more blocks, I passed the park where I played
baseball. Some kids were out practicing. *Must be a Saturday.*
The kids weren't in school.

It was really warming up now and my sock was totally
ripped up, so I took it off and tossed it. I passed several people
who looked me over and walked around me with some
distance. Thank God none I recognized. I finally came to our
neighborhood and paused. So many memories surfaced, many

of them painful.

You've got to try this, Jacob. Keep going. Step, step, step . . . go home.

As I rounded the corner, toward my dad's house, I was immediately struck by all of the cars. The whole street was lined with them. *A neighbor must be having a party*, I thought. I couldn't tell which house was hosting, but I glanced around quickly to see a few people walking down toward the end of the street, toward my dad's house. As I stepped closer, fear gripped me as I considered a funeral, but then quickly diminished as I heard music and some laughter.

I realized that the festive sounds were indeed coming from my dad's house. My heartbeat increased again. *Oh no, I'm going to walk in on something big. What is it? Julia's graduation? Has that happened yet? A wedding? Ben?* I searched my mind to piece together what year it was and how old Ben and Julia were. I tried to imagine what my father would look like older.

I came to the front of the house and decided I would peek around the corner to the back, where all of the noise was coming from, and then, get a feel for what I should do. I was afraid of being seen, and I was trying to keep my script scrolling in my head so I could say it, if I needed to on the spot.

There was some announcement being made from our back porch. I didn't recognize the voice. I peeked around the corner and looked where all other eyes were looking. It was my uncle, my dad's brother, who was speaking and seeming to introduce my father with some nice words. It looked like my father was sitting in his wheelchair alongside him, but I could only see the top of his head. I wanted to see him, but the crowd was blocking my way.

Suddenly, my uncle paused and looked down to where my dad must have been sitting. There was some shuffling of the chairs on the porch, and the crowd began to move in front of me, as if someone was going to come through. I began to see my dad's hand, arched up and out away from him, above the crowd, waving side to side as if telling the crowd to part, as it was doing.

And then it happened. My eyes were instantly met with those of my father's. He was looking straight at me, as if he were looking for me to be there, right at that moment. I froze in shock and fear.

Before I could pull back around the corner of the house, I caught the site of his eyes widening as if seeing something altogether frightening and magnificent at one time. I began to tremble uncontrollably.

The next thing I heard was my father crying out, "Jacob! Jacob!" The crowd quieted, and I heard some rumbling on the porch. "Jacob!" I began to cry. *What should I do?* I couldn't leave. I didn't know if I could even move at that point. "It's Jacob!" he yelled. The rumbling continued, and as I peeked around the corner again, I saw that my father was maneuvering his wheel chair, trying to get through a few people and get off the porch. He was frustrated and bumping into chairs. "Jacob!" His voice began sounding tearful, frantic even. I pulled back around the corner again. *Oh God, how can I face this?* He had aged quite a bit and looked much thinner than I remembered him.

I mustered every ounce of desperate courage I had and turned and stood at the corner. My father was frenzied trying to get off the porch, then without warning, he impulsively leapt from his chair, falling two or three feet off the front ledge and onto the grass, face down. The crowd gasped and groaned. Before people could react, he began crawling on the grass toward me.

I'd never seen or imagined the site of my dad crawling. His arms were doing all the work, with his despondent, long-dead legs, trailing listlessly behind.

Oh, Dad. I couldn't catch my breath or remember what I'd planned to do.

I could see people, out of the corner of my eye look away at their discomfort of watching a crippled man crawl, let alone the host of the party. A few men quickly picked up his chair, ran to him, and helped him get back in. Again, I was frozen. I couldn't move. I could feel that all eyes had turned their focus on me now.

Here it goes, I gathered myself. *Dad, will you forgive me ...* I rehearsed in my mind.

Somehow I was able to step toward him, and he was moving forward toward me with all of his might, now in his chair. I wondered when he would start yelling and lashing out for all of the years I'd been gone, for abusing his money, for leaving my family, for never considering anyone but myself.

As we neared, I cleared my throat. "Dad, please forgive me. I no longer deserve ..." I stopped because I was knocked over. My dad had stopped his chair right in front of me and, with both arms and all the momentum he could muster, propelled himself toward me, coming out of his chair, wrapped himself around my waist, and we both went down.

"Jacob, Jacob, you've come home! You're alive, Jacob." He was crying. Kissing me, squeezing me so tight I thought I couldn't breathe.

I quickly went back to my script in his embrace, "Dad, forgive me. I no longer ..." I tried to get through it but kept getting interrupted by my dad, crying out, "Jacob, my dear son, you're alive, you're home! Oh, my boy!" He was kissing me and crying, and stroking the back of my head. I was stunned.

I was confused and tried again, "Dad, listen to me. Please forgive me. I don't deserve ..."

"No, Jacob, no! You don't need to say anything."

I couldn't take it any longer. I pulled my head back and yelled, "Dad, listen to me!" Our faces were inches away from each other as he continued to hold me tight.

"Dad," I then whispered and cried, "You don't know what I've done. It's bad. You'll hate who I've become." I went limp and began sobbing, as he squeezed me closer.

Suddenly, my father yelled back to the caterers of the party, loudly, "This is my son. I thought he was dead, but he's not! He was lost. Now he's here with us! Go! Get him some fresh clothes and some good shoes from the house. Everyone, this is our Jacob!"

He looked back at me. "Jacob, I'm so glad you've come home!" His eyes were full of tears.

Just then, Ben came up to us and tried to help my dad to his chair. He said, "Dad, you've got to be careful. Let's not rush into this."

My dad pushed Ben off with his arms, and said, "Ben, Jacob is back. We thought he was dead; you know that. We are his family. He belongs here, and now he's home! This party was for my retirement, but now this party is for Jacob! Let's really celebrate this!"

Was he defending . . . me?

Ben either couldn't, or wouldn't, look me in the eye. He turned and walked away, leaving us on the ground.

As I stood and helped my dad back in his chair, I finally noticed my thirst. All eyes were on me. Many were the familiar faces of my past, doing a horrible job concealing their disgust. Ben looked angry, Julia was crying, yet my dad was radiant.

My thirst grew and grew, until I realized that I was going to be sick. And, right then and there, I turned and lost it. I lost it all. All of my pride, my selfishness, whatever I thought I might have to offer to earn something back . . . it was all gone now. I lost my dignity, my composure, and my ability to hide anything.

I could feel my dad's hand on my shoulder, heavy and warm. He was staying near.

When I finished, I was handed a towel, and after cleaning up, I stood back before him. I stared into his eyes, not knowing how to take his undeserved welcome and love.

Thank you . . . Thank you, my tears spoke, as I cried and fell to my knees and lay over his lap.

He was right.

At last, I was here. I was home in a way that I had not experienced or known before I had left. Maybe for the first time, I was really home. My assurance was not about the place where I now stood. Rather, it was about something I couldn't quite explain or understand. It was his love, that's all I could recognize, and his welcome, and his embrace.

I couldn't remember why I ever wanted to be away. It seemed like I had been longing for this sense of arrival my whole life and was now, finally, in its midst.

I sat back on the lawn and put my head in my hands.

I looked up to see my dad wheeling over to my brother who was standing on the edge of the crowd, arms folded over his chest and looking down. I watched them talk. My dad's arms were reaching out to Ben, then one hand rested on one of Ben's forearms. Then, Ben threw up his arms, shaking off my dad's hands. He was obviously angry as he leaned downward and got in my dad's face. He was sternly speaking through clenched jaw and teeth, "Dad, I've never done anything like this to you. Can't you see that Jacob doesn't deserve this? What about me?"

I heard my dad say, in a voice full of tears, "Ben, everything I have is yours ... everything."

I had to look away.

I was bewildered as well. I understood my brother's anger more than I understood my father's love. My dad's love, which seemed to have no limit, no matter what I'd done, was relentless.

I got up just as Julia walked over to me and brought me some clothes, a pair of shoes, and something to drink. She was beautiful. She kissed my cheek and hugged me without restraint, as if I wasn't in the detestable shape I was in. "Welcome home, Jacob. I missed you. I'm really glad you're back."

I found myself holding on longer than the hug lasted. She was innocence and beauty. "Thank you," was all I could say, as I shook my head, took a drink, and looked down at the shoes and clothes.

My father came over to me again and reached into his pocket. He pulled out a very small cloth bag, tied at the top with a drawstring, and handed it to me. I opened it to find another family ring, just like the one I had sold; only this one was polished, unscratched and new. I flipped it quickly to an angle where I could read those words I longed to believe now.

Only this time, the familiar inscription, took more space, and looked longer than I remembered.

I brought it up close to my eyes to read it. Dizziness washed over me. *How did he know? How in the world did he know?*

I exhaled sharply over and over, trying to stave off the coming waves of more tears, as the words that I read settled into my heart.

"You still belong."

Epilogue

I rolled over and my hand landed on something cold and wet which woke me with a start. I could see two large dark eyes staring at me from the edge of my bed. I quickly backed up while inhaling from fear and confusion.

Where am I? What is that?

I couldn't focus and quickly rubbed my eyes, shook my head, and looked hard again at the animal in front of me.

"Charlie? Emma? Is that you?" The now much older yellow lab wagged its tail against the nightstand "thump, thump, thump," as its chin came forward and rested on the sheets just inches away from me.

"Aw, who are you? Charlie?" I reached out and rubbed its head, and laid my head down near the shadowed hairy face and saw the tag on his collar. Indeed it was my old friend, Charlie. I could hear him groan as I pulled him into me and hugged his neck.

I looked around then. *Where am I?* I didn't want to move or mess anything up. I hadn't been in a bed this comfortable in a long time. The house was completely quiet. The previous night was coming to mind now and a wave of awareness and disbelief hit me.

Did that happen? Am I in his house? Did he let me come back?

This wasn't my room as I remembered it, and I began to panic. Without thinking further I reached for my right hand with my left, and grabbed my middle finger.

Yes, it's there. I felt it. The ring was there. I smiled. I hugged Charlie tighter again and felt my eyes water. *Yes, yes!. .. I'm home.* "I'm home, Charlie!"

My head was on Charlie's head as I tried again to take in the room. Nothing was familiar as I looked around until I saw a framed picture on a nearby dresser. Some morning light was shining on it from the window and I could see familiar figures. I got out of bed, picked it up, and brought it back as I climbed back into the warm covers and turned on the lamp next to me.

It was a picture of my dad and me. I was in my high school baseball uniform and he was sitting in his chair looking up at me with a smile that was so familiar and full of pride. I must have been about 15 years old. I was looking at the camera, head tilted with a small smile but I could see impatience and frustration in my face. My heart sank.

What a selfish fool I've always been.

Maybe I shouldn't be here. Maybe he'll have me leave today. It couldn't have been that easy to return, could it? I set the picture down, lay back on my pillow, and grabbed the ring again over my chest as I circled it around and around my finger.

It's mine. He gave it to me again. He said I belonged here. I stared up at the ceiling lost in these thoughts.

I looked around again and saw his shoes in the closet. *This must be his room.* It wasn't as I remembered it. I wondered where he was. I felt alone and concerned about how this was all going to go. Ben finished the night still scowling and upset. My dad stayed near my side the rest of the night and, at one point, even pulled me out on the dance floor with him.

Where is everyone now? I wondered. I rolled over to my other side and burrowed back down into the covers, hoping to regain the assurance of the ring I was wearing.

Once settled on my pillow, I saw him.

He was sitting a few feet from the bed in an old reclining rocking chair with some cushions. He was sound asleep with a slight smile on his lips and a look of contentedness. His head was in my direction. I stared at him. *Did he sleep there all night? Why am I in his bed?*

I kept staring at him, his eyes, his greying hair, and his older creased face. I had never noticed how strong his arms were. He looked so peaceful as I stayed staring from my pillow. His hands were folded in his lap. Then I saw the ring on his finger that was exactly the same as mine.

My hands were clasped just under my chin, and I started circling my ring around my finger again as I kept my eyes on him. As if he could feel my stare, his eyes slowly opened and were on mine.

"Hello, Jacob," he said softly and smiled without moving, eyes sleepy.

"Hi Dad," I said quietly, almost whispering.

He closed his eyes then and fell back asleep. His smile, his eyes, the warmth of his voice, his welcome . . . it all encircled me until I couldn't keep my eyes open any longer and I, too, drifted back into the only kind of sleep you can have when you're completely exhausted, thankful, and truly safe and at home.

The Story of Cole Carson

Prologue

It was after a difficult conversation he was having with his friends.

A group of children was brought to him, in the hope that he might enjoy them and let them come close, but his friends were bothered by this unimportant interruption and began asking the group to leave. To this, he said, "Don't push these children away. Don't ever get between me and them." He continued to explain that children are actually a priority to him and are more likely than adults to receive all that he wanted them to have. He told them that unless they became like children, they would never know or understand anything about him and his ways.

Then he gathered up as many of the children in his arms as he possibly could, and put himself right in the middle of their sticky hands, their sweaty heads, their laughing smiles, and their unabashed love and attraction to him, and they all laughed and fell over one another, becoming a mess.

Later that day, a man of great success and prominence in the community came up to him with a sense of urgency and asked for his advice. This is that man's story. If he had had any idea of the magnitude of what he was asking for that day, he may not have ever asked. But he did ask, and from then on, he was never quite the same.

"Happy birthday dear Cole," the room took in a deep breath and sang its last phrase, "Happy birthday to you!" Cheering, clapping, and laughing all followed the song, sung from smiling faces sitting around the dining room of my favorite French restaurant. Surrounding me at tables of crystal and formal place settings were my staff from our New York offices, some colleagues from around the city, and my wife, Connie, of nearly 25 years.

As we finished our late afternoon lunch they said their goodbyes and expressed their well wishes. I walked back alone after having a brief conversation with the owner who I'd known for years.

Mid-life . . . It's not as bad as everyone makes it out to be, I thought while walking along. *No "crisis." No wishing I was younger. Life is good. I wouldn't change a thing. No major problems. No extreme decisions.*

I waited with a crowd at the light to cross the street. I stood over most of them and looked around. A few colorful jackets, work boots, bags of books, dress suits, phones out, heads down, some mid-30s, clean and shaven, one puffing a cigarette, a beautiful girl, a tired aged man. We all waited until the light changed and then moved across together.

Hands in my pockets, looking up at the beautiful buildings I'd been working amidst for nearly two decades, I was very satisfied. *What a great day.*

As I walked into our office foyer my administrator, Cathy, gave me a smile and a familiar look as her eyes darted to a young man sitting in a chair smiling and looking at me. I then recalled the last minute appointment she had made for me at the end of the day but couldn't remember its details.

"Cole, this is your 4:45 appointment, Mark DiAngelo, representing the Bronx neighborhood initiative," Cathy introduced.

He stood quickly and shook my hand, "Mr. Carson, nice to meet you." *Firm handshake, slightly sweaty.* "Thank you for meeting with me, especially on your birthday," he smiled. He had a boyish grin that softened me instantly. I wasn't in the mood for a funding request, but his navy jacket and freshly ironed pants told me he was.

I responded, "Mark? Please call me Cole. I'm sorry to be late, but please come right in." He followed me through the double doors to my office. As I closed the doors behind us, I caught a glimpse of Cathy looking at me shrugging and silently mouthing, "Sorry." I smiled, turned around and gestured toward the chair across from my desk as I passed by, "Please have a seat. Can we get you anything to drink? Water? Coffee?"

"No thank you, Mr. Carson," he said as he sat down.

I sat in my black leather chair behind my desk and folded my hands comfortably in my lap. "Well Mark, we don't have much time together but please give me the overview of your work and what you are requesting today."

He spent several minutes telling me about the needs and goals of his nonprofit, who was involved, and what their plans were for moving forward. His purpose was clear and his convictions were strong.

"Mark, tell me about your long-term viability. What kinds of resources and support will you need to sustain yourself over years?" I asked in an even tone. I didn't want to overwhelm the young man, who had good intentions and the necessary zeal, but I had to ask.

"Sir, uh . . . Mr. Carson, I mean Cole, you're right, we'll need people who are willing to partner financially with us over a longer period of time," he managed to get out. He continued, "Our annual budget is $195,000 and we already have almost $80,000 pledged for our first year," smiling cautiously, he raised his eyebrows. The grin, again, took effect.

"Mark, I see that you are driven to begin this work, and I think you're the right age and have the energy it will take. Before I can allow the foundation interests to develop with your work, I can only give a start-up amount of $10,000." Another big smile came across his face. "If your work is still going in one year, we can revisit this conversation. The concept is this: The more you prove your worth, the more secure our investment is in you and your future. Does this make sense?" I finished, hoping that my words were understandable to this very nice young man, who didn't seem to have much of a business sense, but I liked him.

As he stood to go moments later, he smiled and seemed satisfied, promising to be in touch with updates on their progress.

Nice guy. He'll learn as he goes. He's green. We'll see.

As I was getting ready to wrap up my day, I reviewed the days' appointments: two conference calls, a meeting with the VP of Human Resources, a late morning appointment with two leading shareholders, more calls, and then the birthday celebration. With a few minutes to spare, I picked up the business section of the morning paper that I hadn't had time for earlier. There was an article about a recent scam discovery, and then a feature editorial entitled "A New Voice on Taxes."

New voice? I wouldn't hold my breath . . . who would have the audacity to think there's a new voice when it comes to taxes and government?

Unable to resist, I began reading.

The writer had attended a public forum held at Georgetown University in Washington D.C. on the topic of "Things That Matter" where they brought together a panel representing the financial, spiritual, physiological, and psychological perspectives.

Apparently the discussion began to focus on the burden of the economy, the ineffectiveness of the government, and the increasing apathy across the nation regarding taxes. The professionals on the panel all took turns responding to the issue of participating in an ineffective system, while maintaining ambition through personal financial means, to impact our own lives.

"Cole, I'm going to head out now. Happy birthday once again. Hope you have a nice night," interrupted Cathy, over the intercom speaker.

"Thank you, Cathy. And thanks for everything you did today. It was wonderful," I remarked while keeping my eyes on the article, holding my place.

I returned to it as the writer gave the summary of each response from the panel members. Skimming now, I read that the psychologist commented on the stress that comes with worrying and doubting your actions and the importance of keeping your physical well being in check. *Expected.*

The panelist representing spirituality commented on transcending the stress and confusion and taking our energies and focus beyond the material world. Meditation, study, and being part of a spiritual community were among the suggestions of what can difference.

I wanted to read how the financial panelist responded to this. *"It's all about risk aversion,"* I would say if I were the one commenting, *"You follow the rules, pay your taxes, even though your belief in the system is minimal to none. In our minds, we need to let that money go and dismiss it. In a sense, that should be our riskiest money, where we require little to no confidence in its earnings. However, with our personal investments, we avoid risk as much as possible, and find ways to secure our money to the highest probability of return."* I could see myself sharing this experienced wisdom in full confidence, ready for questions from all over the imaginary, humbled-by-my-presence room. I smiled at the thought.

About midway through the article, a financial analyst, out of New York, named Jonathan Sanders, addressed the question.

Odd . . . haven't heard of him before.

"Most think of financial wisdom exclusively in terms of return on investment," said Sanders. "An alternative strategy, one that addresses this issue of dissonance in our feelings about our participation with our money, is an approach that keeps in check our values and beliefs in how we use our money. It is a more integrated model of investment. By integration, I mean the concept is more concerned about our very selves being expressed through our money, as opposed to an investment strategy that is separate from our personal lives."

"What about the risks financially, though?" asked a listener, the writer reported.

Sanders replied, "We are wrong to think of the risk to ourselves, as being only financial in nature. There are financial risks on the returns, but there are also far reaching risks to ourselves as human beings when the increase or decrease of our money becomes the sole deciding factor of its purpose. There is more at stake."

What? No one in business could advance like this. Unrealistic. I wonder why this guy was chosen . . . obviously not a hardline Wall Street guy.

Suddenly, a light knock began on my door, and Jim from our public relations office poked his head around the corner. "How about a birthday toast as we close the day?" he smiled. Jim had worked with the company for over 15 years and we had a tradition of sharing a toast on birthdays as the office closed down.

"Sure, come on in!" I motioned and set down the paper. After a drink and a short visit, Jim gathered his things as he stood to leave. A book fell out of his small stack and landed in front of me.

"Let me get that," I reached down and the title caught my eye, *Money That Works.* "How is this?" I asked.

"I just had it recommended to me by Janice from our corporate law firm. So far, so good – I've only read the first chapter," he smiled. "It's a new author, out of New York, so I was curious," he said.

I looked at it more closely and was surprised to see the author was Jonathan Sanders. "Unbelievable. I just read his name for the first time, in an article here in the paper," pointing to it on my desk. I flipped the book over to get a look at him. No photo on the back, or on the inside sleeve.

"No kidding? Well, I'll let you know what I think as I

get through it. Happy birthday Cole, and thanks for the toast. You don't look a day over 85," he laughed. We shook hands. I handed the book back, noticing again the odd coincidence.

✳

From there, I settled into one of my favorite routines.

Once Cathy would leave each evening, around six, she would lock the outer offices, and leave me to what I deemed, my "hour of power." For the first 20 minutes or so, I would wrap up the day's loose ends, finish off any notes I wasn't able to get to, and make myself a list for the next day. Then, after treating myself to a scotch and soda, taking off my tie and unbuttoning the top button of my dress shirt, I would check the closing numbers of the market for the day. I'd been doing this since my senior year in college at Cornell University where Professor George Matthews introduced us to the art of the market. We each began small investments of our own, and began tracing them each day. I'd been doing this just about everyday since, with the very few exceptions of our wedding and maybe the births of our children.

It was about two years after college that I made an investment that changed my life. A company came on the radar over some time that was seemingly marginal and was introducing some computer concepts that many were saying were by far too outlandish.

After an initial risk, over time the stock value increased and I was turning a steep profit. When it was clear that I was a part of something much larger than my experience was able to handle, I went to seek advice from Professor Matthews. He was more than a good professor to me. He became my mentor, friend, and often filled a father-figure role that had long been absent in my life. "Cole," he said to me, "if you do this right, you could achieve a lifetime of financial security, now, in your late 20's." I trusted him, and he was right.

✳

Financial security. My earliest memory of my father was unlike any other of my memories from then on. He was giving me a horsey-ride on his knee, while he was watching TV. I remember I wanted to laugh loudly, but couldn't because he was trying to listen to the news. I must have been 4 or 5 years old at the time.

It must have been a Sunday, because my father worked two different jobs. He sold shoes downtown, as well as worked late night shifts as a custodian. He was hardly home, with the exception of Sundays.

Sundays were the same each week. I woke up to the smell of bacon, which was a treat, unlike the toast for breakfast all other mornings. My mother would feed us all as we woke up, and my dad would eat and then go to the couch and rest for most of the day. I would go and buy a newspaper for him each Sunday, and he would take a long while and read through it.

His scratchy face spoke of his day-off, as well as his ball

cap. The Yankees. He loved the Yankees and wore that cap religiously every Sunday. On Sundays, the smell of coffee filled our apartment throughout the whole day. I can still see his smile as I handed him his paper, and the moment our eyes would meet when he would say each time, "Thank you, Cole, you are a friend and a scholar."

We lived in an apartment in Queens. I was the oldest of three kids, all of us one year apart. My parents had met at an uncle's wedding, at the ages of 19 and 21, were married 8 months later, and I was born 10 months after that. With no education or training, my dad went to work. And he worked, and he worked, and he worked – until one day, when he was 34, he passed out while moving equipment during a midnight shift, and never got up. Apparently, he had a heart condition without knowing it, and at the age of 12, I lost my dad.

Within a month after his passing I began working and, like my dad, never stopped. I joined my mom, who had just begun working for the New York Times. She worked the 12 to 7 a.m. shift, folding and packaging papers for delivery the next day, came home got us to school, slept all day, woke to feed us dinner and put us to bed, then went back to work. I began delivering papers when I was 13, continued stocking newsstands and stores, then began managing routes, all while going to school.

I didn't think about it, I just worked, like my parents, and helped wherever I could with my younger brother and sister. I worked so hard I excelled in both work and school, and never had much of a life otherwise. I graduated high school at the top of my class. I worked for a year prior to college, applying for every bit of financial aid I could find, and to my whole neighborhood's surprise, was accepted and admitted to Cornell receiving scholarships which made it possible.

At college, my pace of working hard continued. Professor Matthews called me into his office one day, just after our senior final projects had been submitted. "Cole, your project is the best work I've received in years. I want to congratulate you on an incredible college career," he offered.

My lungs were full, my head spinning. I exhaled, "Thank you, Professor. That means so much coming from you," was all I could muster.

"Cole, I want you to be around for the long-haul, achieving great success with that drive and work-ethic of yours, and making the world stronger economically than we've yet known," he looked me in the eye, lending me all the confidence he had to give. No one had ever at that time, or since, spoken so convincingly into my future.

That was enough to usher me full-speed forward into my career, and on into my present hour-of-power routine . . . where I was finishing yet another day at the office, in the same manner I had year after year. It was like breathing to me . . . opening my portfolio on my computer, checking my investments, entering the numbers into my spreadsheet, watching my margins adjust, deciding the changes I wanted, emailing my broker those changes, and getting a new sense of hope and excitement about what returns those changes might bring the next day.

✳

I always had to watch the clock. I had made a promise to Connie that I would leave the office no later than 7:30, and I was always surprised at how quickly that last hour slipped by. I had so much energy for this I wished I could do more of it during my daytime hours.

With the commuter traffic mostly under control, I was able to walk in the door by 8:15 at night, with time to check-in on the kids and tuck them in bed. Connie and I had our dinner after that together, as usual, talking over the day's events. After the dishes and kitchen were cleaned, we settled on our comfy twill couch, that Connie recently found and loved, to watch an earlier recording of the nightly news. We both were news junkies, and enjoyed this 30 minutes together at the end of our days.

"I'm going to get a drink of water, want one?" she asked as she got up about half way through.

"Sure, thanks, want me to pause it?"

"No, I'll be right back, go ahead."

The next segment was about young entrepreneurs who were making unusual profit gains, contrary to the current economy. It focused on the recent years' success stories. When asked who were their current influences, one answered, "Jonathan Sanders." That's all, the story moved on.

What? I rewound it, and pressed play. *"Jonathan Sanders,"* it repeated. *Him again? Who is this guy?*

"Honey, come here," I called out. She returned, glass of water in hand. "Listen to this." I rewound to the beginning of the story.

"Yeah, what is so big about that?" she asked.

"Jonathan Sanders. Have you ever heard of him?"

"No. Should I have?"

Connie was also involved in the financial world, unlike many of my colleague's wives. She had a degree in business herself and actually had worked with me in our earlier years, creating and managing our foundation. She was also part of a women's investment group, who sought to develop and manage their own portfolios. We were a good match, and often spent time, even during our vacations, researching or visiting new investment opportunities.

"Based on my day today, you would think so. This is the third time I've come across his name, all referenced as an accomplished person in the financial world. How could we not have heard of him yet?"

"Jonathan Sanders . . . no, not familiar to me," she concluded, and then took interest in the next segment on the current national unemployment rate. But, I remained fixed . . . *Jonathan Sanders*. I decided to look him up the next day.

※

I walked up to my building at 7:25 a.m., right on time. I passed by Patty, a mainstay who sat on the ground off to the left side of the front doors.

"Any spare change, Sir?" she asked as usual. Her eyes were downcast as she raised a cup out in front of her, toward me. Her threadbare, stained pink gloves clenched the cup, which contained two nickels. Her bags were stacked on either side of her, containing her possessions. She sat on a newspaper, unfolded out underneath her things.

I reached in my pocket and dropped in the three quarters I had as change from the toll bridge. As the coins clinked against one another, she began slowly raising her gaze, but I was already past her entering the door before we caught one another's eyes. "Thank you, Mr. Carson," I faintly heard her say.

I entered our floor moments later. "Good morning, Cathy," I said, as she handed me the paper and my daily café Americano, as she had been doing every morning for eight years. She was the best assistant I'd ever had, and was well worth the extra 20K I offered, to persuade her from her former job. She matched the competency of many of my executives, and then some.

"Good morning, Cole," she warmly replied in rote. "You'll begin with an 8 o'clock call from our San Francisco Executive Team."

"Thank you," I whisked by her, right on schedule.

Just like the hour of power to close the day, I enjoyed

this 30 minutes nearly as much, in that I could use the time however I wanted. I took a sip of my coffee, opened my laptop, checked the opening stock numbers, and then quickly typed in and searched "Jonathan Sanders." A page worth of sites popped up, beginning with his website for his book, followed by his appearance at Georgetown recently covered by the Post. I clicked on that, where it had a link to his online biography.

Jonathan Sanders. Notre Dame undergraduate studies, Harvard Law and Business Schools for double graduate degrees, taught at international locations in the Middle East and Asia for Harvard, while also entering the business world as first an investment banker for five years, followed by his current role as a consultant, writer, and speaker.

Back to the search page and down two entries, was his blog link, titled "It Could Happen To You." I clicked it, realizing I was racing with the clock to learn what I could before my 8 o'clock call began. It was as if I were doing a word or number puzzle being timed, trying to feverishly piece together this mystery of a person.

His website was fascinating right from the start. There was an image of a boy, who through some advanced graphic programs morphed into a man, who morphed into many different images of men from different races and cultures and ages, and then back into a boy . . . all taking about 30 seconds.

"Cole, San Francisco is on the line and ready," Cathy called in.

"Cole?" she asked after I didn't respond right away.

"Yes, yes Cathy. I'm here, it'll be just a minute more and I'll pick up. Tell them I'll be right with them."

I clicked on the link to his travel schedule and speaking engagements. He was going to be in New York on February 6th. I looked at the calendar quickly, that was in one week. I would be returning the night before from meetings at our Midwest regional office.

"Cathy, will you please get me a ticket to hear a 'Jonathan Sanders,' who is speaking on February 6th at the Hyatt in Manhattan? And, please reschedule any conflicting appointments that day if needed."

"You want to go too, huh?" she sounded surprised.

"Who else is going?"

"My brother was telling me about this last week," she said. Cathy's brother worked for NBC in the city, and over the years we had had occasional professional conversations across many topics.

"Oh, is that right? Well, yes, please look into it and let me know what you find. I'll take the call now," I said, and switched the line, "Jim? Alex? Sorry for the delay."

✳

One week later I walked into the Grand Hyatt Manhattan, 15 minutes before the presentation was to begin. I'd been to many of these events throughout my early career and had been the keynote speaker a couple of times myself. I gave my admission ticket to a young man at the door, who looked a bit nervous amidst this crowd but smiled his best and politely welcomed me. I picked up a glass of water at a table in the back and then proceeded to find a seat near the center of the room, to the left side. The familiar air of pride, success, and a confident posture filled each suit and every aisle as I cut through the crowd. It was a sea of black and navy, nice ties, high heels, smart scarves, clean cuts, and shaven faces.

The session started right on time, and the emcee introduced the speaker as one of the more surprising current voices in the business world, primarily due to the fact that until fairly recently, he hadn't been well known in the public arena.

Nice to know I'm not the only one.

As the applause broke out, bringing him up on stage, I sat upright hoping to get my first glance and impression. I saw him as he took his final step onto the stage. Sharply dressed in a dark suit, white shirt, and burgundy tie. He was clean-shaven, had brown hair, and was a little over six feet tall, all very average so far. He shook his host's hand firmly and routinely, and set a few things on the podium. He then took a step off to one side, came around to the front corner of the podium, and over the next 20 seconds or so, he went from one side of the room to the other, seeming to catch eye contact with several people and when he did, he would nod slightly and flash a warm and somewhat knowing smile. At first I thought he was acknowledging those he knew in the audience, but when I saw his eyes cast both from the front to the back of the room, and even once to the young man who took my admission ticket who was now standing at the front right corner, I realized his unique greeting was indiscriminately landing, ready to acknowledge anyone. The room began to quiet, and ready itself for what was to come.

He returned to stand behind the podium, took a sip of water, and then began: "Hello friends. Thank you for having me here today. It is an honor and a privilege to have a few moments to share some ideas that are having some impact amidst my associates. I hope you'll enjoy this time to consider these ideas, as well as have the capacity to envision them for yourselves on some level," he paused.

"Before I go further, I need to tell you, that when I was at Harvard, I was part of a type of loose fraternity of fellow students who gathered for nonsensical relief of academic pressure every Friday night. We did everything from poker nights to karaoke at various Boston pubs to spontaneous road trips, not knowing where the adventure would take us. One such outing, found about six or seven of us in New York City walking into this very same Grand Hyatt Hotel with no particular purpose in mind but to find some mischief," he smiled and paused, as the room lightly laughed, and began swelling with some anticipation.

"The first thing we did was take the elevator to the top floor to get the lay of the land and to buy us some time to figure out what to do. Just before descending, we found ourselves alone, with the exception of one guest: a distinguished looking, elderly gentleman in his 70s dressed to the nines. He seemed to have come from a late evening meal at the very chic restaurant on that floor. As the doors closed, without second-guessing myself, I called out, 'Silent trousers,'" he paused very effectively once again. The room waited, pregnant with curiosity as to what this meant. "What you need to know is that this was a common code for us to drop our pants and stand in our boxers with no words exchanged or laughter," laughter began in the room, and I found myself liking this guy.

"So, we did so, without saying anything, stood there, pants around our ankles, watching the elevator numbers descend, making for an uncomfortable and awkward ride for our new elevator hostage. We had a couple of stops at the top floors," a loud laugh came from the back somewhere. "The doors would open, we would stand as if nothing were unusual, move aside a little for the new person, however, inevitably they would decline either in laughter, or with a look of disgust, or perhaps fear," again more laughter. He came off the podium now, and we all eagerly followed him along, "All the while, our elderly elevator passenger who was now our accomplice, stayed completely silent, never broke a smile as his eyes took in our behavior. Friend or foe, we wondered as we began descending to the lobby, the ultimate challenge for our prank lying ahead. Without any hint or word, at about floor 9, he silently dropped his trousers and stood awaiting the final plunge, in solidarity with his newfound brotherhood," the room roared. Jonathan began laughing with us as well.

"We were used to holding in our laughter, but once our new team member joined us, a whole new challenge was on!" he laughed. "So, we reached the lobby, the 'ding-ding' of the opening door rang, and we stood our ground. The waiting guests and bellman were there to greet us, eyes looking up and down taking in the gravity of the situation, which for some was more obvious than others," he shook his head, as we exploded, "If it weren't for our newest member standing at the helm, we would have surely been escorted immediately from the building as a young group of college boys; however the stature of our obvious front and center captain could not be contended with, and the doors closed in silence. Our leader pressed floor two, reached down, pulled up his trousers, fastened them, and exited quietly. Just before the doors closed, he turned and said, completely seriously, 'Gentlemen, nice doing business with you.'" The room broke out in laughter and applause.

"That was the last time I was in the Grand Hyatt. I assure you today, however, that I will keep my trousers on," more laughter, "unless, of course, I hear the code words!"

From there Jonathan Sanders introduced himself, his background, and some of his early experiences, which were fairly ordinary, yet told with certain winsomeness. He was very amiable and I found myself thoroughly enjoying him and glad that I stumbled upon his travel schedule. From his time in the Middle East and in Asia, he shared some fascinating perspectives that were a refreshing challenge. He closed with some ideas that he had hinted at in the coverage of the Georgetown panel discussion, which entailed viewing our money and what we do with it, whether in risk or in security, as something that is integrated with the elementary principals of who we are as a person.

I wondered at this again. I no longer interpreted his thinking as young idealism. After hearing the depth of his thoughts and experience in business and in the greater world however, I couldn't quite follow his purpose in turning the conversation to this seemingly personal level with a group like us listening.

As he closed, the crowd stood and applauded showing their appreciation. Someone yelled out, "Silent trousers!" He laughed, paused, began to unbuckle his belt then waved it off as we all laughed together.

As I often had done in the past, I made my way to the front, hoping to meet him and thank him for his presentation. Often when I did this, and introduced myself, people recognized my name and we would spend some moments appreciating one another's accomplishments. It was a way of networking in some cases, but more, in this instance, I was interested in getting to know him or possibly even scheduling a follow up appointment.

In a room like this, it was not surprising that many others had the same idea. I decided it was worth my time and found my place several people back in a line waiting to meet him. I watched him through the shoulders and heads of the group who encircled him. Many had a copy of his book for him to sign. He was quickly responsive and personal with each admirer but kept the pace moving. When it came my turn, I extended my hand, "Mr. Sanders, Cole Carson, I wanted to tell you how much I enjoyed your presentation."

When I said my name, his expression changed a bit, "Cole Carson, nice to meet you. I was wondering when our paths might cross. I have followed your success for many years now. Please call me Jon." He smiled warmly, took a step closer, and placed a hand on my shoulder as we continued shaking hands with one another.

"Well, I must say that your name has been recurring quite frequently in my world as well," I replied, "and I was glad to have the time to come and hear you today. I find your experience combined with your perspectives fascinating, and I'm looking forward to reading more of your work."

"Thank you, Cole. That's very flattering coming from you. I hope that I won't disappoint you," again the warm smile. Our handshake had stopped moments ago, but his hand still remained on my shoulder.

"Cole," he lowered his voice some, "What can I do for you today?"

"For me?" I smiled, glanced quickly around, uncertain of his question.

"Yes, Cole, for you. What did you have in mind?"

I stalled and checked my watch, configuring my reply. His deliberate question threw me off center a bit and caused me to respond candidly. "Well, Jon, I am curious about your philosophies, particularly where you intersect money practices with personal values, and if you're asking, I wondered if we might discuss this more thoroughly over lunch sometime," the yielding tone in my voice surprised even me, as I suddenly recognized a sense of reverence for this man.

"Yes, Cole, we can do that. I would enjoy more discussion on this as well and would consider it a privilege to do so with you," he comfortably said. "This is a common conversation I have with people of your caliber and experience with investments."

"Thank you, Jon, I'll look forward to hearing more from you on this," I safely concluded.

A long pause.

"Well," I rushed, awkward with what to say next, "I'll have my assistant get in touch with you to find a common time in our schedules?"

He flashed another smile and nodded quickly, "That would be great." He looked down now and took a small step closer, turning his head to the side, speaking quietly to my ear, "Cole, is there something more you'd like to ask?"

"Excuse me, Jon?" I replied, leaning my ear in toward him.

"Was there more, Cole?"

Aghast, and suddenly lost in this conversation, I

searched for the handle or wheel by which to gain control. I
didn't know where to go with this. I pulled out my
handkerchief, said, "Excuse me, please," and faked some
coughing while turning my shoulders.

*Think, Cole, think. Just say, "No, there's nothing." Is there
nothing? What is it? ...*

As I was refraining from eye contact for the remaining
seconds within reason to stall, suddenly, and strangely, I knew
he was asking something I could answer, but couldn't find the
words just yet.

I glanced around, there were only a few others who
were waiting now, and were probably hearing some of this.
Normally, I would end this and walk away, but nothing in me
wanted to do this now. I turned to look at him squarely, and
his eyes were patient despite his persisting questions.

I took a deeper breath . . . and instantly knew.

"Jon, you're the reputable expert here, what can I do to
be totally secure? Both in terms of concluding my life in
financial good standing . . . and," I searched for the words that
I was at that very moment becoming aware of myself, "and . . .
morally speaking."

This question caught me so off-guard and was so real
that it suddenly pressed into my chest and caused my
breathing to become shallow. I would have been fearful
except that as I spoke to him, I had an utter sense of peace
while asking.

He smiled. He nodded.

"Cole, it's interesting you call me an expert in this regard. I would say, only God himself is the expert of morals, but you already know what keeps you in moral good standing: a faithful marriage, practicing your life with high ethics and integrity, honoring those ahead of you," he answered simply.

But this was somehow too small of an answer. "I've done all of this, Jon," I said, as he looked down. "Since I was a boy, I have always followed the rules and have held high rapport in all of the circles I've been in," I proudly said with a nearing sense of angst. I was bewildered at where this had quickly and urgently come from inside of me. Now it was my hand on his shoulder, calling his eyes back to mine, "Jon?"

He waited, looked into my eyes, and nodded slightly again, "Yes, Cole. I see this is true of you."

It wasn't enough though, and now it was my turn to press, "But . . . what?"

He took in a breath as he put his hands in his pockets. He slowly exhaled, and leaned closer again, "Cole, one thing is missing."

My eyebrows arched in a silent question, imploring him to go on. A small smile sneaked across my face, relieved that an answer would be revealed.

"Cole, sell everything, and give it to the poor. Then, you'll be secure forever. And, then also, start following me."

He wasn't smiling now, and neither was I. His eyes were locked firmly on mine.

"Excuse me? Say that again, please?" was all I could say.

His eyes buried themselves deeply into mine, and leaning in just a bit, said again, "Sell everything you have, Cole, and give it to the poor, and follow me."

My hand dropped off his shoulder. My vision became blurred so I rubbed my eyes, and searched the room for something to bring into focus . . . anything. I was hearing my breathing as if through headphones with too much volume, magnified and loud. Moments passed, as the outline and details of chairs and people beginning to clean the room became defined again. I returned my focus on him. He stood, still next to me, solidly unfazed, holding his gaze on my eyes.

Then, an unprecedented sense of sadness overcame me as I became aware of my inability to respond to this request. There was no way that I could consider what he was asking. Something felt nonnegotiable and terribly certain like receiving the shocking news of a friend's sudden death, or a crushing diagnosis.

My eyes began stinging and a moment later a tear dripped off my cheek and onto my hand. I wiped my eyes again. I saw the few remaining other people waiting, uncomfortably turning and looking away as they became aware of what they were seeing.

"Cole," he said, but I didn't respond. "Cole, listen, it is really hard to come by the security you're trying to acquire, while being wealthy. Some might say that it's easier for a car to fit through a coin slot, than for a person of wealth to be truly free and receive the accomplishment of good standing with God."

"Impossible," I heard one person whisper to another nearby. Another one interrupted and called out, "Well, then, who can do this?"

I had stepped backwards a few steps, bumped into a person, and was turning away now. I felt dizzy. I felt weak and nauseously unstable. As I tried now to regain my balance, heading toward the door to get out of the room, I heard Jon respond, raising his voice some, "I know what you're thinking . . . impossible. However, just because it is impossible for us, doesn't mean it's impossible All things are possible for God."

Walking without looking, I bumped into a woman on my way out the hotel doors, spilling her coffee onto the lobby floor. Normally I would stop to help and apologize profusely. I could only glance at what had happened and kept stumbling forward, anxious to get out of the building. Once outside the doors, I called for a cab and rode back to my office, seeing nothing around me. *What just happened in there? What's going on?* The sadness dissipated and out of desperation, I began to see how ludicrous his response truly was.

Anger started its crawl, as a fog bank moves in over the ocean's shoreline.

How the hell could he expect me to even entertain what that would do to my life, my business, my family, and all that I've worked for? He didn't answer my question at all. There is no security in making oneself poor. I've been an upstanding citizen in every way, and have no reason to question myself morally. That was presumptuous to infuse God's approval or disapproval into the conversation. Who does he think he is?

My fists and jaw were clenched and pulsating. I was in a sweat over the public embarrassment of the scene. I regretted approaching him personally at all.

I was dropped at the curb, paid the driver an unseemly tip without caring, and made my way up the elevator to my office on the 16th floor like a horse who goes barn sour and races to it's home without a thought. Cathy said hello, and asked how the time went, and I distantly said it was fine and abruptly disappeared behind my door.

In the safety and privacy of my office, I sat at my desk for a long while. I poured myself an early double scotch. I leaned back and stared without focus at the ceiling, searching, wondering. The lines in the ceiling contour . . . the circular lighting fixtures . . . the window shades, partially pulled and slanted. I was suspended in time, wondering. Looking around hard, searching for something for my mind to grab, something that would ground me.

He knew. He knew that the question existed in me, because once I asked it, I knew it was mine. How did he know that about me? I just met him. How was he so confident in his response? It's totally unreasonable. Who can possibly end their life secure, if they give everything to the poor?

Lines. Shapes. Vents. Bookcase. Computer. I scanned them all as if looking for some clues they might give me, all the while sitting dumbfounded in my comfortable leather chair.

The emptiness of losing my father so long ago was

close, and inescapable, as tears streamed down my cheeks, first silently, then with startling gasps for breath.

Why now? This isn't fair. I picked up the phone to make a call, but didn't know to whom, and hung up. I got up and paced the office, watching my shoes . . . step, step, step. I sat back down. *Am I supposed to fight and work as always, or give in?* I couldn't think.

He asked for the impossible from me. I can't do that. I won't ever be able to do that.

Moments, minutes, and then an hour or more passed without focus.

Suddenly, I couldn't handle it.

I stood up and threw my glass across the room and seethed as it shattered against the bookcase. I hit the call button, "Cathy, cancel the rest of the day for me."

"Cole?" she quickly replied, "Are you okay?" Her voice was fearful.

"Yeah, I just need a break. Sorry for the noise. I'm fine. I'll be back on by the morning. Take the rest of the day off yourself. Go surprise your kids." I didn't want any questions.

"Okay, Cole. You sure?" she asked.

"Yes, I'm sure," I said.

"Okay, I'll get my stuff together and see you tomorrow," she let it go.

I'm done.

For the first time in years, I turned off my computer at 4 p.m., turned off the lights, and locked the door. I went to the gym two blocks away and had an unrelenting urge to run. I got on the treadmill at 4:25 and ran blindly for over an hour, staring out over Madison Ave.

The running, the drum of my feet, the pound in my chest, the heave of my breath, all seemed to be the only working and sorting out I could manage.

✳

As I drove up to the house early for the first time in years, I saw Connie's surprised, and then concerned expression flash through the kitchen window as she watched me drive up.

"What's wrong?" she came out to meet me, drying her hands on a kitchen towel.

"Nothing," I smiled, "Nothing's wrong. I decided to come home early today. Can't a guy surprise his wife?"

"Not you, Cole. Come on, what's happened?" She wasn't thrown for a minute.

"Hey, you know what? I decided I wanted to change gears today, for a lot of reasons that we can talk about, but nothing for you to be alarmed by. Can you just let me come home and change gears?" I pulled her to me and gave her a hug, and kissed the top of her head. "Really, can we just do that?" I pressed and slightly pleaded.

"Sure Hon," she conceded. "Sure." She backed away to get a look into my eyes, and I held her concerned gaze for a few seconds before looking down to grab my briefcase.

We walked in silently, with my arm around her shoulders. "Nice sunset, huh?" I noticed aloud. Walking inside, Connie went to the bar and poured me a drink, and I thanked her.

The agitation resurfaced again after dinner, once the kids were in bed. I poured myself a gin and tonic and offered one to Connie, but she declined. I watched the nightly news in silence and wandered in my thoughts throughout the various news updates.

I was exhausted by the wavering emotions that I'd been swimming in all afternoon, and had another drink while Connie was getting ready for bed, desperately wanting to be done with this day. As we turned out the lights and kissed goodnight, she said, "Cole, you've hit the bar hard, huh? You okay?"

I patted her shoulder as I drifted off, "Just let me come home Connie, just for tonight, just let me come home." I was asleep in minutes, or maybe seconds.

✳

I was falling . . . falling . . . falling down and somehow found myself sitting in a classroom desk in high school. My dad walked in the classroom and called me out to the hall. "You didn't get the paper," he scolded me. "I will, I will," I ran out onto the snowy sidewalks looking frantically for the paper. I was looking so hard, "Where is it?" I was yelling, but no one was hearing me. I walked in a door and Connie and the kids were all seated at this really fancy restaurant dressed up singing, "For he's a jolly good fellow, for he's a

jolly good fellow ... " "Stop, stop," I yelled, but again, no one could
hear me. "Where's a paper for my dad?" I screamed. I was on the
sidewalk again and saw the newspaper, in a machine, and I searched
my pockets for change, turned them inside out desperately. I was on
my hands and knees, running my fingers under the machine,
looking for a coin. A rich man in a business suit walked by and
flipped me a coin; I was 12 again. I was pushing the coin in the slot.
I could see the paper behind the glass. The coin didn't fit. It wouldn't
fit. It was too fat. I couldn't fit the coin in the slot, and I was
hysterical, "Get in there! Get in there!" I yelled. I slammed at the
machine. I tried to shake it. I picked up a rock and broke the glass
and cut my hand but grabbed the paper and ran, and ran, and ran,
but not fast enough, because I came up to the ambulance just as they
were carrying my dad away. "No! No! I got you the paper Dad. It's
right here!" The blood soaked newspaper now fell. And that hand
was on my shoulder again, and I turned and saw Jonathan Sanders,
and I was 48 again, and I was instantly mad and hurt, and yelled,
"Why? Why everything? Why do you want everything?" ... His
eyes stayed kindly on me, and I started to cry, and cry, and cry, and
I fell into a ball, in my suit, in the snow, at his shoes, and he knelt,
and I tried to say, "I love you, but I love you Dad, but why
everything?" ... Then panic swelled as I heard my heartbeat build
and build and build, and I kicked and I tried to breath as I felt
squeezed, and pushed, and squeezed - but couldn't be relieved, and I
had to scream, I had to scream, "No! No more! No, I don't fit! I can't
fit! Stop! Stop!"

Connie shook me yelling, "Cole! Wake up! Cole!
Honey! You're having a dream, wake up!"

Perspiration soaked through into the sheets, and I was
trying to get my breath, and I heaved and heaved, and then,

"Oh God, oh God, oh . . . " I reached out and clenched her in
my hands, grasping for anything real.

"Cole, I'm here, I'm here honey," she was trying to calm
me. I fell back on my pillow, regaining my breath, rubbing my
head.

"Oh God, Connie," I whispered and moaned. I pulled
her into my arms.

"I'm here Cole, it's over . . . just a dream," she whispered
and wrapped all of her around all of me, trying to blanket my
fear with herself. I began drifting back to sleep thankful not to
be alone.

※

I woke the next morning feeling hung over and in a
terrible mood, completely attributing the nightmare to my
drunkenness, avoiding as much of Connie's concerns as
possible.

I've got to get back on track today, to my routine. I drove to
the office in silence, no morning news and no music. To that
point in my life, I could count on one hand the memorable
dreams I'd had. This one now topped that list. *Get back on
track today, Cole. Get ahold of yourself.*

Patty was asking for change, in her same place to the
left of the building doors. Her stench was stronger than usual,
and I noticed a fresh cut on her forehead as she looked down
at the ground, while raising her cup in request. I tried to
imagine where she would have gotten that cut. *Did she fall?*

Was she hit? Had she been cut? Someone had stopped to drop in some change, so I took the chance to pass by them both quickly, and walk inside.

Another time.

As I logged onto my computer at my desk moments later, I decided to first check our foundation's quarterly giving activity, instead of the opening stocks. It was at 1.22 million. *Was that enough?* I decided after looking over several R & E reports of the company that we could increase the foundation giving to 1.27 million over the course of the next fiscal year. It would be a loss of 1.7% of revenue for the company, transferred over to the foundation, but I figured it would be minimally felt by myself or our offices, and would probably only impact year-end bonuses already slated to be at an increase this year, to everyone's delight.

Feeling mildly satisfied, I grabbed an empty leather journal in my desk that Cathy had given me for my last birthday, and noted the change I'd just made: "1.22 to 1.27 increased foundation giving." I closed it and slid it into my bottom drawer, next to my bottle of gin.

I took several calls that morning, sat in on two executive level interviews for hire, worked with Cathy on a partners' communications piece we were getting ready to release, then was getting ready to walk out for lunch when Cathy called in, "Cole, Mark DiAngelo is on the line for you."

"Who?" I asked.

"Mark DiAngelo, from the non-profit group working

with neighborhood teens who came to see you recently?"

"Oh, right. Did he say what it was about?" I was ready to eat.

"No, just that he wondered if he could get a minute with you to give you an additional figure that you would be interested in."

"Uh . . . okay. Put him through," sighing, I plopped back into my leather chair.

"Mr. Carson?" he broke in.

"Cole. Yes, hello Mark. What can I do for you?" I cut to it, hearing my stomach growl.

"Cole, thanks for taking my call. I wanted to quickly update you that we were given a recent gift of some size that I thought you would be interested in."

A *sizable gift?* I wondered what that meant in Mark's naive and simple terms. "Oh? Wonderful. You must feel encouraged!"

"Yes, it was an anonymous gift actually, and I wanted you to know about it with your recent questions of our viability in mind," he explained.

"Anonymous gift? That's interesting," I said, thinking of the tax write-offs lost in foregoing a documented gift. "Was it given by a long lost wealthy relative?" I smiled facetiously into the phone.

"No. We don't know the source. The name it was given under is unknown to us," he explained.

"You have no idea where it's come from?" I had a

hard time believing this.

"None at all," he replied. "It almost sounds like a spoof in title, but we checked it out, and have actually already cashed the check of $195,000 to our account, so apparently it's legitimate." I could hear the smile in his voice; he was obviously enjoying sharing this information. I recognized the annual budget amount, and was sincerely happy for the vote of confidence this must be for this young man.

"Spoof you say?" I asked, "Why do you say that?"

"Well, the account it came out of was titled M.S. Trousers," he said with a slight chuckle.

"Trousers? Is that what you said?" I asked.

"Yeah, strange huh?"

I was leaning forward, without knowing, staring into the small desk speaker where Mark's voice was coming from. *Is that a last name? If not, who uses the word trousers? Who uses it except . . .*

"Cole?"

"Yes, strange. May I ask what bank that came from, Mark? I have many friends in the banking world, it would be nice for you to be aware of the source of this charitable gift, perhaps we can find out," I said.

"It's First National, Cole. But frankly, I don't want to pursue knowing who it's from if they've worked so hard to remain anonymous. The exact amount, when cashed, closed the account as had previously been instructed. So, whoever gave us the money, wants to remain unknown," he concluded.

Maybe so.

"Well, good for you, Mark. Thank you for letting me know. Send over a letter of this conversation to my assistant, Cathy, and she will make further arrangements with our foundation, for an additional $10,000 gift." I said, uncharacteristically without much thought at all. It was a gut feeling, I went with it, and immediately it felt right.

"Cole, thank you so much! That's very generous of you. I'll send that along right away. And, Cole, you won't regret this. You should see the steps we've already made in the community with a few of the families."

"Alright, thank you for your call, Mark," I said without hearing much, ready for my sandwich.

After preparing for a few days of travel to our Chicago offices, I left for home right on cue at 7:30 p.m., feeling back on track. After getting on the freeway, I turned on the radio for some news highlights of the day. I always enjoyed sinking into the news, and breaking away from the work of my day, no matter how unsettling the reports were.

※

Chicago had record-breaking cold temperatures, which kept me inside and tense the whole time away. All was going fantastically with our company there, and our people were thriving in unprecedented ways.

Returning to my office again, I sat down to the paper and the note scribbled to myself before I left: "M.S. Trousers."

I hadn't forgotten about this, and decided to ask Mike Timmons, who handled some of our accounts at First National.

At 9:00 a.m., I asked Cathy to get Mike on the line for me. "Mike, how are you doing over there with all of that money?" I smiled. It's how I'd greeted him over the phone for over 15 years.

"Hi Cole. I'm just rolling around in it as usual. What can I do for you today?"

"Well, I've run across an unusual situation in working with a nonprofit start-up and consulting with them on some of their finances," I stretched the story easily, "and wondered about an anonymous gift they've received from an account with First National."

"Yes," he said, with some unease.

"Not to worry, I'm not wanting any overarching private information, but wondered if you could help with identifying the full title of the account? It's listed as M.S. Trousers." I proposed.

"Trousers? As in pants?" he asked.

"Yeah, that's right," I waited.

"Let me look into it and see what information is available."

"That would be great. Thanks Mike." We finished, and I set the note aside.

✳

Two days later, Cathy had Mark DiAngelo's letter on my desk, which summarized the conversation we had previously had, as well as thanking me for the additional foundation gift. A receipt was attached, with the tax ID number for our filing purposes. I was impressed with Mark's timeliness and communication. I suddenly became very curious about his work and was interested in visiting the shelter, or wherever it was that he operated from, I couldn't quite recall.

Cathy located his contact information and arranged for me to meet him the following Friday for a site visit.

My driver dropped me at the front steps of North Bronx High School where Mark met me at 3 p.m. that afternoon.

"Hello Coach," I said to him, as we shook hands.

Mark smiled easily, "You like this look, huh?" His t-shirt said "North Bronx Football" and he wore a whistle on a lanyard around his neck. "The team is around back on the fields, we can walk this way, " he lead us through a side corridor of what must have been the administrative offices. "This is one of the roughest schools in the city. The dropout rate is over 24 percent, one of the highest in the country. Crime and violence right up there as well."

I became increasingly aware of my surroundings as he spoke. Two cop cars were parked along the chain-linked fence lining the far side of the football field. Gates to certain hallways and classrooms had been locked for the day. Multicolors of paint swatches coated the gymnasium exterior walls, from layers of covering graffiti over years it looked like.

"Monday through Friday, I come out here to help coach their football team. Two-thirds are on academic probation. Six of them are on active parole. Eighty percent come from broken homes, mostly without fathers," he quickly gave me a snapshot.

"Hey Coach," said Number 38.

"Hey Jones, looking good today," he patted Jones on the shoulder pad. "Jones, this is my friend, Cole. Cole, this is Travell Jones, our lead running back."

"Nice to meet you," he said as we shook hands.

"Likewise," I said.

"Cole, practice is over in 20 minutes. Are you okay here on the sidelines for a bit?" Mark asked.

"Sure," I said. I watched as he jogged out to the huddle with two other coaches and the players. He patted a few other players as he approached, and they nodded and said "Hey Coach," in reply.

I stood, hands in my pockets, taking in my surroundings, which were totally foreign to me. I could have been in another country for the way that I felt at that moment. I'd been a New Yorker all my life, and never would describe this setting, the kids in front of me, or what Mark was describing, as my hometown.

Tattoos, long hair, shaved heads, angry faces . . . clusters of kids over on the corner outside the field, by a market, looking suspicious . . . cops keeping an eye on them . . . two girls walking up to the field, girlfriends watching maybe, one of them pregnant . . . the smell of marijuana from somewhere nearby. Mark, in the middle of the field, "Hey, nice play, way to go line!" Smiling . . . hitting helmets and pads . . . a few players smiling through helmets . . . more of them looking angry and resentful, a chip on their shoulder. It all was a foreign country to me.

The practice ended and Mark ran over and said, "Are you hungry?"

I wasn't, but I said, "Sure," for some reason. Mark told some players that he would meet them outside the locker room in 15 minutes, and we walked to his van, and drove over to meet them at the door.

The van was about 15 years old, and two colors of blue, with threadbare tires. Against my better judgment, I hopped in the front seat. Me in my suit, and four big boys packed in the back, made our way to a nearby pizza place where Mark ordered six pizzas and pitchers of sodas, which were all gone by the time we left. I insisted on paying for the food, then went to sit down where Mark was sitting in the middle of them, and waved me over to the empty chair at their table.

Mark was probably about 30 years old, white, educated, tall and lanky, maybe a basketball player in his day. I paused before I sat down, taking in the scene, and how unusual it was to see someone like him in the middle of boys like them.

As we were finishing, Mark said, "Cole, we all made a

bet while you were paying for the pizza, about how much your suit cost," he admitted and smiled. The boys all smiled a little sheepishly that Mark let out their secret. I smiled.

"I said $1,000," said Jones. It was a little quiet.

"Higher," I went along with it.

They smiled and leaned in, "$1,500?" "$2,500?" "$2,200?"

"Bingo," I said. High-fives all around.

"Shit," said a kid named Javier, "$2,200 for a suit!"

I was laughing too. Mark laughed easily and made no apologies for them. He suddenly said, "What about this? If Cole went and sold his suit, and gave one of you the money, and said the only requirement is that you needed to spend it on something important in your life, where would that money go for you?"

"That's a lot of weed," said Jones, and they all laughed again.

Obviously, this wasn't unusual for Mark to throw out a question, because they responded pretty easily, and I was surprised. "I'd pay my uncle off for my dad, he's always threatening him," said one.

"Pay the rent for my mom, and maybe my aunt too," said another.

"Pay my girlfriend's doctor's bills, at least 'till the baby comes," said a kid they all called "Hub Cap." As he said this, one of the guys next to him elbowed his arm gently without looking at him. Another one nodded, while letting out a shallow sigh.

Mark was folding the paper that came from his straw; all eyes were fixed there.

"There's lots of things we'll spend a couple of dollars on here and there, without thinking, but somehow when you have more, you think about the potential of what it could be, for important reasons," commented Mark, "Seems like you guys have some important things in mind, I like it." And that was it. Mark said let's go, and we loaded back in and dropped off each player at various housing projects throughout the Bronx, then Mark drove me to meet a volunteer who worked with him.

Her name was Stacy and she was about to finish her shift at the Boys and Girls Club. It was an old grey cinderblock building with a sign over the door with blue and red block lettering. We were waiting on the steps outside the door when a few girls were pulling up to the bike rack along the wall to the right side. They were riding old pink and red scratched bikes. They looked about 12 or 13 years old. They were in the midst of a conversation as they got off their bikes and then one said something to the other, and they broke out into loud laughter. This continued on as they walked by us and through the metal doors. Both Mark and I smiled at hearing them.

Just then, Stacy came out and gave Mark a brief hug, and we shook hands as he introduced us. After she told me a little about her role there at the Boys and Girls Club, they both shared stories of getting to know kids in the community and building friendships with them.

"We feel that in order to have any impact in their lives, we need to prove ourselves in a sense of real friendship first, so we spend time with them, in their world, in ways where we can get to know them," she explained. Stacy was a small young lady, with magnetic large brown eyes, full of energy. She was clearly well educated and capable. I wondered how her path had lead her here and had no doubt that if anyone could ambitiously take on making a difference in this community, it was people like Stacy and Mark.

"What do you mean by impact?" I casually asked, not sure that I understood exactly what their purpose was all about.

Stacy flashed a glance at Mark with raised eyebrows, and he dipped his chin to her. "Well, I would say the impact would be multi-level. Overall, with any kid we meet, we are hoping to deliver hope and encouragement on some level. Deeper than that, we would hope that they would feel genuinely loved. And beyond that, that they would come to know of the source of this love that is bigger than just us," she summarized.

"What about impacting the conditions of their lives? The projects? The crime? Pregnancies," I pressed, "Is this part of your purpose as well?"

"We would love to see the conditions of their lives improve and hope that they will, but I guess we have grown to see that if they first feel loved and connected to purpose for their lives, that these things will more likely follow for the best reasons, as opposed to first focusing on behavior changes," Mark added, as he took a sip of water from the bottle, finishing the conversation. Our time was up.

Instead of calling my driver for a ride back downtown, Mark wanted to drive me back and said he had a stop to make anyway.

As we returned to the downtown area, it was fast-paced and the streets were full of suits, heels, taxis, horns, lights, and energy. The city was crazed with this pace, as usual, people moving fast in every direction, constantly. With every turn, closer and closer to the heart of the city for me, my mind's pace picked up and returned to the many things left undone in my office that afternoon.

We reached the curb and, turning, I said, "Mark, thank you for your time, and for . . . educating me, to your work," I smiled and extended my hand.

"No problem, Cole, and thank you for taking the time to come and see," he warmly responded. "A different world, huh?"

"Yes, absolutely." I opened the door and it creaked a bit. Through the open window, I asked, "What shape is this old beast in? Are you able to keep it up and running well enough?"

"So far, so good!" he clearly wasn't complaining. "I'm going to try and get it in for the 150,000 mile tune-up in the next months, then we should be good for another 100,000."

"Go do it tomorrow, and I'll pay for it. Call Cathy in the morning and she'll have it covered," I patted the hood and waved goodbye.

"Thanks Cole. Have a great afternoon and evening," he pulled away from the curb with a jolt, hopping into the rushing stream of traffic. I noticed the right taillight was out, and decided to tell Cathy to have that fixed as well.

Patty had fallen asleep on the ground, sitting up against the wall, to the left of the building doors. The temperatures had dropped, and she was all wrapped up in a big grey jacket, a red scarf, and yellow beanie. Her cup had tipped over, with what looked like about two or three dollars worth of change spilled on the ground next to her scuffed, brown work boot she was wearing on her left foot.

I paused from a distance as I approached.

Without thinking further, I went to her, bent down and scooped the change back into her cup, and added $20 to it, then tucked it inside her arm, facing toward her, so that it wouldn't spill again.

✳

My evening was what I feared. Too much to do in too little of time. I walked in the door at home at 10 p.m. Connie was just finishing the news and looked exhausted.

"Hi Connie. So sorry I'm late," I kissed her forehead.

"Yeah, we missed you here tonight," she said curtly,

"What kept you?"

"I decided to go and take a look at one of our smaller foundation works, and the time got away from me. I had to stay late at the office then, to get tomorrow's numbers ready for a 7:30 a.m. call."

"You can call you know," her tone was cutting.

"Hey, you know how things go sometimes, Connie. This visit this afternoon was really kind of amazing for me," I was now following her down the hall, talking to the back of her head. "Connie, stop, please look at me," I reached out to hold her elbow from leaving. She turned, face full of something I didn't recognize.

Suspicion. She didn't believe me?

"Cole, I'm tired. Days are long for me too. And frankly, this isn't like you. You are a clockwork kind of guy. You don't deviate from your planned schedule, ever. This, and that dream you had recently, have gotten in my head lately, 'I love you, but why everything' is what you were screaming in your sleep," her eyes were hurt and resentful. "What's going on Cole? Is there anything you need to tell me? Is there someone getting your attentions?"

"No. No. Not at all, Connie. God, no!"

"Then what's going on inside of you, Cole? You need to be honest with me, and put some words to this, because I'm becoming weary of interpreting what I'm looking at!"

Her voice was intense and abrupt. I was infuriated that she would question me. For a moment I wanted to shake her, then turned sharply away, and headed to the bar for a drink. As I poured myself a glass-full, I heard her in our room. I had to collect myself. My anger was scattered and without focus, but I could feel it. I sat in my chair, and decided to watch the news by myself, not minding the message I was sending, and hoping to calm myself down.

Once it was over, I walked into our dark room, got ready for bed, and slipped in the covers, hearing Connie's wakeful breathing.

After several minutes, I finally said, "Connie, it's not what you're thinking. Something is going on for me, but I don't know what yet. It's not another woman."

"That's good to hear."

Another several moments passed.

"Do you think you can put anything into words then, to help me understand?" she asked.

I let out a heavy sigh, "I'm not sure. In fact, that's what I'm feeling . . . not sure."

"About what?"

"About life . . . about my view of it. About how I'm experiencing it," I struggled.

"Are you unhappy?"

"Yes, I think so, in some ways. And then in others, I feel like I'm just getting glimpses of something different. And, for some reason, it scares me . . . like I'm missing something."

Several minutes passed. It was hard to know where to go in the conversation from there. Then, slowly, she turned toward me, reached an arm over my chest and let her head rest into the familiar nook of my neck and whispered, "Okay, that's all I need to know for now."

I patted her arm, sighed deeply, and said, "Thank you."

✳

Two weeks passed in a heartbeat. Connie and I returned to our comfortable rhythm, and even spontaneously added in a weekend trip to Martha's Vineyard with the kids. The fresh air and beauty were mind-clearing, and helped us regain our focus on our goals we had shared for years and years together.

Our company secured a record-breaking purchase of a smaller company, ensuring an overall profit increase within two years. Despite the economy, we were one of the few thriving companies, and I was beginning to feel back to my old self again. My routine had returned, and Connie and I enjoyed the confidence and ease of our pace and tempo.

It was in the third week that once again, unsettling things happened.

I was walking quickly to grab a sandwich for the 30 minute break I had, and wanted to get some fresh air. There was a deli a few blocks away which I had my mind set on.

Suits, heels, horns, cabs, lights, traffic, faces, more faces, mostly looking down or away. We all rushed to get there, and then get back. Some checked watches. Some checked phones.

Some talked to someone in their ear. Laughing, swearing, telling, complaining. The city was a dressed-up ant-farm, not really much different.

As I passed the Federal Building, I noticed a handful of people near the entrance, and others quickly walking and looking in that direction. I curiously walked that way to see what the commotion was about. Just as I reached the edge of the group, I saw the doors open and out walked Jonathan Sanders. The small crowd was roused a bit: "Hello Mr. Sanders" . . . "There he is" . . . "Is that him?" whispers could be heard.

Amazing. My jaw dropped. I was stopped in my tracks at the coincidence and sense of excitement in the air. He waved, smiled at a few people and shook some hands, as he progressed out of the building and toward the street. I was hidden behind a few people, out of his view.

As he neared the street, he suddenly stopped and for no apparent reason turned and looked over his shoulder, and up at the building. With all eyes on him, we followed his gaze and noticed a man sitting in the window on the second floor, watching. It got a little quiet all of the sudden, with a few whispers, "Who's that? Why is he looking up there?"

Jon waved at the man, who immediately seemed embarrassed to be seen so publicly. Responding in an apologetic wave, his eyes went from unabashed curiosity when we first looked to self-consciousness at our noticing him.

Next, Jon motioned for him to open the window. The glass framed man acted like he couldn't understand, but Jon made it emphatically and awkwardly clear that he wanted him to raise the window. Some of the crowd yelled it out then, "He wants you to open the window!" The look of risk was all over his face. He reluctantly lifted the window, with more effort than one would imagine was needed.

It got quiet. The city was never quiet.

"David! Come down here," shouted Jon.

"What?"

"Come down here, David. I'd like to talk with you, and go to your house," Jon smiled.

Shock on his face. Fear. Embarrassment again. Then, slowly, a very slight, nearly unnoticeable smile.

We all seemed to be holding our breath, unsure if it was safe to exhale, or maybe nervous that we would miss something from the noise of our own breathing.

David and Jon's eyes were locked on each other for about five stern seconds, and then David threw down the window, and rushed away. Moments later he was running through the door out to Jon. No jacket, no briefcase. Just him, right up from his desk it seemed.

"That guy is a son-of-a-bitch," said a man next to me to his friend, "That's David Cohen. Works for the IRS in their corporate division. He's single-handedly taking down small businesses right now."

I could've been mistaken, but it sounded like a few

people actually were lowly booing when he came through the doors while others spoke hushed profanities.

I had read about him in a couple of articles over the past months. I had noticed that he was getting slammed in the editorials. He was clearly mistrusted. I didn't envy his position.

The crowd's very recent excitement was now silenced at the atrocity of this sudden invitation. Jon was a respected man; David was a hated man.

Why? Why would he associate with someone like David Cohen?

Chills began up and down my spine and a wave of nausea swept through my stomach. I numbly backed up a few steps out of the crowd and found a seat on a planter's edge. Staring down at my feet, I could hear their cab drive off and the crowd disseminate.

"Can you believe that guy? How did he get Jonathan Sanders to befriend him? He's such a fraud," the crowd complained as it walked away.

I sat there in confusion. My heart raced, as my increasing anxiety returned. My stalwart truss of confidence in myself was waning. I was once again disarmed by confusion and this feeling of being unsure about . . . everything. I hated it.

"You okay?"

I looked up to a young man in his 30's, in a suit, hands in pockets, shading me from the sun with his tall frame.

"Uh, yeah, I think so. Just feeling a little under-the-weather."

"I was watching you during that spectacle that just happened. Are you as disturbed as you seem?" he smiled and invaded my space and head at the same time.

"I guess I am," I decided not to fight it.

He sat down next to me and said, "My name is Randy Jordan. I'm a friend of Jon's."

I looked him over quickly and sharply, "Yeah?"

"Yeah."

"Well, Randy, what do you make of that scene then?"

He laughed lightly and shook his head, "Well, with Jon, you never know. He is both unpredictable and consistent at the same time. I don't know anyone else like him."

"You got that right," I conceded with some exasperation. "What's he doing mixing with a guy like David Cohen?"

"I'm not totally sure, but like I said, he's consistent. Recently, he also befriended Walter Grayson. You know him?"

"Of course," I said in paralleled shock. Grayson was the epitome of a crooked bureaucrat in the city. Any upstanding businessman knew of his dishonest and self-serving ways.

"Well, shortly after their meeting, Grayson held a big dinner party for Jon at his house. You should have seen who was there: known duplicitous businessmen, their escorting women and men of hire, high-end drug dealers, flamboyant fashioners, and the list goes on. All sitting together, with Jon in the middle. Wonderful food and wine, loud and boisterous talking and laughing. Didn't feel right at all that Jon was in their midst."

I was dumbfounded. "Right. So, what was going on? Why would he subject himself to those associations?"

"Exactly, that's what we were wondering," I assumed he meant others like him, who counted themselves friends. "Some of us finally pulled him aside and asked, 'Why? Why are you partying with these people?'"

The crowd was completely gone now. The city had resumed its feverish pace and bustle around us, yet our conversation had my full attention.

"What did he say?" I had to know.

"He said something from left-field. He said, 'I'm not needed by the honest and ethical; it's the ones who struggle who need someone to reach them differently.' Then, he turned and continued with the party. Jon's marching to the beat of a different drum, one that often doesn't make sense."

"What keeps you around, then?" I asked. I glanced at him again next to me. Dressed impeccably with a nice hair cut. His hands were loosely clasped, elbows resting on his knees, looking down at the walk below him.

"I don't know really. I just know that something is different about him. No one else seems to have the width of audience he seems to be speaking to, and he's just a great guy," he simply concluded. "I need to get going. What did you say your name was?"

"Cole. Cole Carson. I hadn't said." I shook his extended hand. "Thanks for talking."

"Take care, Cole," and he got up and left.

I sat there a while longer, until sound by sound, the city built it's roar in my head again. I suddenly realized the time, and jumped to my feet to return to the office, without ever getting my lunch.

※

At the close of the day in the office, I decided to find any recent news on Jonathan. I was surprised to see so many current posts on him, all since I'd first looked him up not so long ago. I looked quickly at who submitted them: the New York Post, The New Yorker, NBC, and CNN. There were a couple of links to articles referring to some kind of dispute with city zoning and the location of commercial sales: "Sanders puts business permit freeze on suspected wrongful profiteering," it said. Then something about "the misuse of church properties not intended for market sales." One article tag implied a heated public conflict.

That's hard to imagine. Must be the media spinning the story.

I kept scrolling through the search results and saw several that didn't fit with the rest. The Globe. The Star. Tabloids.

"Homeless man says his blindness was 'healed'!" I

clicked the link.

"Bart Callahan, a homeless man in New York City for the last seven years, said that he was 'miraculously healed' of his blindness last Saturday while sitting near the Metro station entrance at 86th Street and Lexington, one of his frequent panhandling sites," it said.

Ahh . . . the beauty of the tabloid article.

"I was sitting there, as I usually do, with a sign and cup for hand-outs. I heard a crowd coming and yelled out, 'What's going on? Who is this?' Someone yelled back, 'Jonathan Sanders, get out of the way. Move your feet!' They were idiots, but I figured he must be important," said Callahan.

The crowd of about 50 people had gathered quickly following the celebrity siting, while Sanders was leaving a nearby restaurant, wearing a Valentino suit, with two assistants at his side. "I kept yelling out, 'Help me! Mr. Sanders, please, help me!" Callahan remembers.

The crowd suddenly came to a halt, recalls Carmen DeSoto, a neighborhood passerby who works at Josie's Night Prowl waiting tables.

"I didn't even know who we were following at first, but I didn't want to miss what was going on. We stopped so fast that I stepped on the man's foot next to me with my heel. We had out our phones, trying to take pictures, people were whispering, some were yelling to shut up. It was crazy," said DeSoto.

Sanders stopped in front of Callahan and was heard to say, "What do you want me to do for you?"

Bobby Torino, a delivery boy for Papa's Pizza, watched and said, "It was strange. The dude with the suit seemed like he wanted to help, but we all knew that this blind guy had been around begging for years . . . good luck at helping him."

Callahan was heard saying, "I want to see."

"We all had a good laugh at that one," said Torino, "then Sanders bent down, and out of nowhere said to the blind guy, 'Then, see.'"

"We all got quiet, and whispered to the back what he had said," remembers DeSoto, who was clearly upset. "Then the blind guy started looking around differently, and it was like a horror film! 'Oh my God! Oh my God!' I was yelling. He started reaching out his hands as if he could see Mr. Sander's face, then he started looking at all of us!"

Reports of screaming and shouting were told. "I've seen this homeless guy around this neighborhood for years," said Torino. "He's a certified blind guy! All of a sudden, he was seeing! It was the craziest thing I've ever witnessed. Scared the living daylights out of me."

Sanders quickly got up and left the scene, getting picked up by his black Lincoln Town Car. Callahan had to leave the area as well, "What is a guy supposed to do? One minute I couldn't see, the next I could! I got up and was ready to celebrate, but most people were backing away from me in fear. I went from one kind of a freak to another. I had to leave."

The photos were typical of tabloids, a little out of focus, like they were discreetly taken. Jonathan Sanders was in a photo out of context, probably some speaking engagement, caught in a posture and expression that could be seen as preaching with the caption "Businessman or healer?" And another picture of Bart Callahan that looked like a mug shot, clearly seeing now, and focused.

A tabloid article of a healing? They'll print anything for a story! I refused to process it. I wished I hadn't read it at all.

I closed my laptop and turned my chair. I had to get my eyes out and away, out somewhere else. I stared out the window to the sky, the big blue sky. I was lost; I was reeling with thoughts; I found the building lines against the sky and traced them with my eyes, from the far left to the right . . . up, over, down, up, over, down . . .

I was feeling so conflicted about him. Although the idea of Jon healing someone was beyond belief, I couldn't discredit his astonishing bold ways entirely. He possessed an unusual confidence and a type of authority with which he consistently seemed to function.

Just then, Cathy interrupted on the speaker, "Cole,

are you there?"

"Yes," I said.

"Mike Timmons is on the line," she clicked off.

I picked it up quickly and gladly left my unsettled thoughts behind, "Mike, how are you doing?"

"Hi Cole. Doing well. Staying busy. You?"

"Same. What can I do for you?"

"Well, I found the account that you'd asked me about. The full title is Matthews Silent Trousers."

The phone slipped from my hands and dropped loudly on the desk.

"Cole. Cole are you there?"

Picking up the phone, I held it out away from me for some moments. "Cole?" his small, distant voice called me.

"Yes, Mike. Yes, I'm here. Uh . . . I uh . . . I'm not sure I understand," I stammered.

"Oh, did you not hear me? The account name is 'Matthews Silent Trousers,'" he repeated.

"Yes. Yes. But, Mike, what I don't understand is this title on the account. What does that mean . . . to you?"

"Oh, Cole, I don't know. People use account titles for all sorts of reasons. This one sounds like an inside joke. But, who knows?" he finished.

"Okay, okay Mike. Thank you for getting back to me. Are there any other details to the account? Anything at all?" I was reaching, trying to wrap my mind around the potential conclusions.

"No, not really. Just that the account was terminated upon the payment and amount that you brought to me initially. I guess it could be interesting that the account was created almost five years ago, with that amount, and no activity occurred until it was recently terminated."

"Did you say five years?" I asked, "Is that common?"

"Yes, five years. For a discreet account like this, it's a little unusual. Usually these types of accounts are set up, and then moved along fairly quickly, and dissolved, for whatever intended purpose it began in the first place."

I stared without seeing out my office window. *What are the chances of this being a coincidence?* I suddenly felt exposed somehow, or followed. *Was someone? . . . Was Jonathan Sanders?*

"Cole, is there anything else I can do for you?" Mike said.

"No, no that's it, Mike. Thank you very much. Take care," I finished. I hung up, searched for my alma mater and old professor, and immediately dialed.

"Cornell University," the co-ed cheerfully greeted.

"Professor Matthews please," I requested.

"Just one moment," she replied.

After being there for nearly 35 years, Professor Matthews was very well known in the College of Business and Economics. "Matthews," he abruptly answered. He was the perfect combination of a salty old dog with a brilliant and zany academic flare. His voice betrayed years of pipe smoking and the confidence of his age.

"Professor Matthews. It's Cole Carson, how are you doing?" I couldn't help but find myself smiling as I heard his voice.

"Cole! Good to hear from you. I'm doing alright, just up to my nose in grading final projects, but what's new? And how about you? What can I do for you?" he offered, as he always had.

"Well, I'm looking into something a little unusual, and it's a long story, but let's see . . . I'm wondering if you happen to know a Jonathan Sanders, a businessman here in New York, or if the words 'silent trousers' mean anything to you?" I put it out there and cringed at the absurdity of my question as I spoke it aloud.

"Jonathan Sanders? Yes. I know of him, and have read some of his recent works. Interesting guy. Good thinker. Silent trousers? Is this some kind of joke, Cole?" he quipped.

"No, although it could be and I just don't know it. So, do you have any personal history with Sanders?" I probed.

"No, never. Just have been following his career. Is there anything wrong, Cole? Your voice sounds a little different," now, it was his turn to probe.

"Uh, no, I'm fine, thank you. Just perplexed is all," I trailed off.

"Well, that's unusual for you Mr. Carson. You are the most consistent, reliable person I know in the business world. Wish I had more time, but I have a class starting in five minutes. Anything else for now, Cole?"

"No, thank you, Professor. And take care."

"And you as well, Cole," he concluded, as I slowly hung up the phone, lost in thought.

Without clearly deciding to do anything, I decided to do nothing. I didn't actually want to pursue finding out anything more. Maybe I wouldn't know for sure if there was ever a specific connection between M.S. Trousers and Jonathan Sanders and Mark DiAngelo . . . and me. It was disturbing to me, and somehow I came to the conclusion that there was wisdom in leaving this alone. And so, I did.

※

It was two or three weeks later, as I was arriving at my office in the morning, that I noticed something new to me in the city. Two blocks before my last turn, as I sat waiting at a light, I saw a delivery truck backed part way into a driveway. On its side, it said: "Concerning New York: An Investment with Significant Rewards," and its back door was open. There were people gathered around the truck being given grocery bags of food it looked like. What was noticeable was that those handing out the food looked to be businessmen and women dressed in suits, ties, heels, and jackets for professional jobs, likely beginning in the next hour.

I drove into my building's parking structure and decided to look them up, as I often did when something got my attention. Just as I was entering the lobby, I recognized a woman coming in the front door who I'd just seen at that delivery truck. She was dressed impeccably: patent leather shoes, a slate grey jacket and skirt. Her appearance was full of confidence and determination, like many of us working in this building.

I couldn't help myself.

"Excuse me," I called out.

She looked my way, didn't recognize me, and continued to the elevators.

I moved closer, "Excuse me, can I ask you something?"

She carried the day's Wall Street Journal, and a file that looked to be pulled for a morning meeting. I quickly assessed her to be in her 40s, very physically fit, and a sense of competency rang loudly. "Sure, what is it? I'm afraid I'm running late though," she said quickly, glancing at her watch.

"Of course, I understand. I'll get right to it then. I believe that I saw you at a site nearby, seeming to be handing out grocery bags just now. Is that right?"

"Yes," she smiled briefly and nodded. "You're right. That was me."

"Can you tell me what that is about? 'Concerning New York' your truck said?"

"I can't say much right now, but we're an investment group. You can find us online." She reached in her purse and handed me her card. "Give me a call if you have any questions, and I can get you whatever you need regarding our portfolio."

"Gretta Wilson," I read out loud. She nodded. "Okay, thank you Gretta."

"No problem. Are you Cole Carson?" she suddenly thought to ask.

"Yes, I am," I said curiously.

"Ahh, I was told I would run into you sooner or later, nice to meet you," she warmed, and seemed paused, making some kind of associations with my face in her mind. It made me feel a little awkward.

"Mutual colleague possibly? In the building?" I asked.

"Possibly," she smiled and stepped into the elevator, closing our conversation, and left me behind in the lobby.

"Concerning New York," I whispered as I looked at the card. Something didn't match about her, but I had a meeting in 45 minutes that needed my attention now, so I put the card in my wallet, and waited for the next elevator.

❋

The holiday season was fast approaching, which meant that all former margins of down time were coming to a close. Connie and I had had a Christmas shopping tradition for years that included both work and play. On a Friday in November, she would come and meet me in the city, and we would begin with dinner together at our favorite restaurant, Daniel, in the Upper East Side, between Madison and Park avenues. We'd been going there for years and usually made our reservation for the next year as we left each time.

We would then stay overnight in the city at the Plaza Hotel right off of Central Park. The next morning, we were a force to be reckoned with as we hit all of our shopping at once: family, friends, and the company and foundation's clients and employees. Christmas was a huge endeavor, to put it mildly. We shopped for two days straight and had most everything sent to my office, where Cathy would receive it the next week, sort it, and prepare the timeline for all wrapping and deliveries. It was easily half of Cathy's job during the months of November and December.

In addition to all of the gifts, this year we were also treating ourselves and our kids to a trip to Fiji for Christmas and New Year's. The kids had been looking forward to it for months, as had Connie. I was happy that they were happy, and lounging on a warm beach with a cool drink in my hand didn't sound too bad to me either.

It was particularly relieving to have had such a successful year-end quarter occurring for the company. We were up by eight percent, with numbers still increasing. We were feeling the ease and liberty of spending, which was always more enjoyable.

It was November 3rd, prior to this year's holiday shopping weekend that Gretta Wilson's card fell from my wallet as I pulled out a credit card to pay for lunch with one of my executives. "Concerning New York," it read. "Gretta Wilson: Venture Investment Partner." Still remembering the curiosity I had upon meeting her weeks ago, I decided to give her a call, just after lunch, impulsively.

"Cole Carson," she came on the line after her assistant

put me through. "I was wondering if you were going to follow-up with a call from our brief meeting."

"Hello, Gretta. Yes, I'm following up. I've been bombarded with business, but haven't forgotten meeting you, and keep finding myself a bit curious about what this 'Concerning New York' is all about."

"Good, glad you called. We are actually having a partners meeting a week from Thursday, just after work, if you would like to come sit in and see what this is all about?"

"Oh, I wouldn't want to intrude," I backed away.

"No, not at all," she interrupted me. "This is how I learned myself. The group is open to those interested in learning more."

"Well, can you tell me a little more about your group in general? I mean, I saw you on the truck that morning, before work, and have read some from the website, but what is all of this exactly? Is it a religious group, or non-profit charity work?"

"Well, let's just say, we're a highly ambitious group, interested in high risk, high return collective investments," she said matter-of-factly. I took note that few people used the words "high risk" so comfortably.

"So, feeding the homeless from the truck, I'm assuming you're a non-profit, right?" I repeated.

"Actually not. We're for profit. But that is something you're going to have to take another step to really understand. Can you come on that Thursday evening?" she asked again.

"Well, you definitely have my curiosity, but I will readily admit, I have a pretty steep risk aversion, so I can't say that I see exactly why I should take another step," I chided, feeling relieved at the clarity of mind I felt, at least on this.

"Yes, Cole, I can imagine that you manage your risk very carefully and successfully; however, I also imagine you to be a man who understands rewards quite well, and I would like to appeal to that aspect in you and challenge you to come and see for yourself what it is that our group is committed to."

Bold. She drew me in.

The silence was thick for about five seconds before I gave in, "Well, alright, I'll see what I can do. Where are you meeting?"

"The Press Room for drinks and appetizers at 5:00, off of Madison. There is a back room that we're meeting at, so just head back there, and I'll have a seat for you," she said warmly.

"Oh, okay, alright. I'll try and make it," I concluded.

"I hope you will. The meeting will last about an hour, and then, if you have time, it would be good to have you sit with one or two members and myself, to further clarify who we are and answer any questions you might have," she finished.

"Okay, very good. I'll plan to see you then," I said.

"See you then."

✳

Almost two weeks later, I opened the door of The Press

Room, which was a small, upscale pub, well known for the frequencies of both famous, and not-so-famous news reporters. The back room looked full from a distance, but I caught Gretta's eye and then her wave to me to come back and join them. After getting a drink and meeting a few people, I tried to take a seat near the door, hoping to have an out, should I need one, however Gretta directed me to a chair near her at the far side of the room.

The meeting opened, with some updates of what they called "existing investments." A middle-aged man named Paul reviewed a project called Restoring Life which supported the rebuilding of functional lives of ex-cons with housing, a job, and a community. It appeared to be a networking project, along with some touches of personal care and support. Paul concluded, "So, I think we've impacted approximately eight percent of this year's former inmates now released into the public arena from the county prison. Our goal for a year from now will be ten percent." He smiled.

There was a small round of applause, along with "That's better than where we were at last year," "Way to go, Paul, thank you for being the point on that," and "At least some are making it out of the system."

Next, a woman named Nancy was introduced to speak about an investment in the Bronx for a neighborhood medical clinic, serving residents without insurance. Nancy was sitting to my far right, near the door, and as I turned to look her way, I was shocked to see Jonathan Sanders sitting next to her.

I didn't know when he came in the room, but I'm sure he wasn't there when the meeting began. I was overcome with a flash of sweat and kept my eyes downcast. I was afraid of having eye contact for some reason. As I slowly allowed my eyes to return to Nancy, I could see that his focus was on her as well. And so I locked my eyes onto her, committed to keeping my eyes off of him in the event that he might be looking my way at any point.

Nancy's report was remarkable. The group had already purchased a building and hired three full-time physicians and four support staff. The doors of "Bronx Medical" had been open for six months. Altogether, over 1,100 patients had been treated. "So," continued Nancy, "we're reaching about 27 percent of the need in that neighborhood and plan to increase that by one additional staff and 475 additional patients by next year."

Again came the applause from the 30 to 35 people in the room, along with similar encouragements shared aloud.

My eyes traveled everywhere but in his direction.

There were two more reports given on existing projects: the renovation of a condemned church building in a highly populated African American neighborhood and food distribution to the homeless, which is what I had observed that day.

Next, there were two proposals for the group to consider as new investments: A center for people with disabilities, where different therapeutic professionals would treat clients, as well as support services for families, and, restoring a neighborhood park that the city had proposed to do but didn't have the funding for.

I continued my gaze elsewhere, continuously.

The meeting closed, just as Nancy sneezed, and I reflexively looked her direction to notice that Jonathan Sanders had left and was no longer in the room. I looked around, but he was nowhere to be found.

Gretta leaned over to ask, "Cole, do you have a few more minutes to talk?"

"Uh, yes, I believe I do," I said.

"Okay, let's meet in 5 minutes at the booth to the left side, just outside this room," she quickly planned.

A few "partners" came over and introduced themselves. I recognized one or two of them from different affiliations of the past and from the business community. As I made my way to the booth, I continued to look for Jonathan, but he had apparently left.

When I arrived, Gretta was there with one other gentleman, who stood as I approached, "Hi Cole. My name is Steve Patterson. I'm with IBM and have been part of Concerning New York for six years now. Glad to have you here tonight." He shook my hand warmly.

"Nice to meet you Steve. Thank you for having me," I slid into the booth across from them both.

"So, what did you think?" asked Gretta.

"Amazing! Absolutely amazing," I smiled, and let that

stand on its own for a bit. "I've never heard of a group taking on this kind of work from the business world. In fact, why haven't I heard more about you?" I sincerely was puzzled.

"We are intentionally under-publicized and have gone to great lengths in our arrangements with the city to protect our investments by minimizing attention," explained Steve.

"Yes, but what about the contagious effect on the community? Seeing the goodwill of others and having it rub off on the public?" I countered.

"As a group, we've decided otherwise that the complications caused by the attention ultimately can do harm to our clients and exposes ourselves in a way that might inhibit our continued involvement, which also hurts our clients," Steve articulated.

"Okay. Fair enough. It's your right and your investment," I respectfully concluded as I leaned back in the booth.

"Tell me what is drawing you all together, or how do you ensure your returns at such a high risk level, like Gretta has been telling me about?" I decided to get to the point.

Steve and Gretta gave each other a quick glance, and Gretta began, "Cole, we don't have this conversation with many people, and once we have this conversation, we are going to ask you not to mention it to anyone outside of our group, but we do allow spousal disclosure."

"Well, that's nice," I laughed, going along with the joke, and taking a stiff drink of my scotch. When I looked up from my drink, I knew one thing … it wasn't a joke. "Really? What are you talking about?"

"Are you in agreement with that request, Cole? Would you be willing to sign something right now that you will not speak about our group's terms to anyone outside of the group upon hearing them? We know it sounds severe, but you will see that it is necessary for the protection of our purpose and values," Gretta said unwaveringly.

"Why do I get to even hear the terms then? Aren't you breaking code now?" I was trying to downplay the sudden seriousness and outsmart them, but knowing I wouldn't.

"Because you noticed us, you asked about us, you pursued more information, and you're a candidate due to your potential contribution profile," she answered.

"Because I'm rich? Is that it?" I was a bit contentious due to the alarming way I was being lead into this conversation.

"You are of means, absolutely, but we don't contact anyone about us, we only respond to inquiries, and if the profile matches, we are free to share our terms," Steve chimed in.

"Well, what if this is as much as I want to know? I'm not sure about this secrecy stuff, when I'm not sure exactly what you're going to be telling me," I again protested.

"Then, the conversation can end right now, and we thank you for coming and hearing about our investments and hope that you will be discreet in not referring to our group in connection with these endeavors," Steve kindly, and patiently, said while taking his last sip of what looked to be a glass of merlot.

Gretta, too, finished her drink, and waved to a few partners leaving the room next to our booth. The Press Room was dimly lit, but the room was full of people coming in after work.

"Can I think about it?" I asked.

"Sorry, Cole. Our format is that upon delivering the offer to hear our terms it is a one-time opportunity. Again, this is to protect our group and our ventures, not to apply false pressures on anyone. Also, you should know, that you will be offered an opportunity that you can accept or decline, and both are completely fine with us. So, there's a chance that you'll hear our terms, decline to participate, and simply walk away and only be obligated not to repeat our conversation," finished Steve.

Why wouldn't I let them tell me now? I can accept or decline. I've certainly been in the middle of that proposition hundreds of times in business. How bad can it be? They are respectable, upstanding business people, the virtuous projects, and ... he was in the room.

"Okay, where do I sign?" I made light of giving in, although I felt my hand tremor a bit as I pulled out my pen.

Gretta pulled out a paper from her briefcase. It was simple and straightforward, and I signed and dated it easily.

"Okay. Let's hear it," I looked at them both squarely.

I didn't expect what I heard next. In fact, not in a

million years would I put together what Concerning New York and their partners had committed to.

"Cole," began Gretta, "we are a group of professionals, who have committed to high risk corporate investment, based on some very unorthodox principles, that travel into the moral values we share."

I held my focus, and nodded slightly, encouraging her to go on.

"We have each agreed to sacrifice our personal assets, of a common percentage, indicating that we are committed and that our values are consistent amongst us," she was nicely paced in her disclosure.

Sounding cultish. Where is this going? I again nodded signaling to continue.

"To be specific, Cole, each partner, has entered into our group contributing three quarters of his or her personal assets," she kept her face straight, her eyes riveted on mine, rivaling all of my internal thoughts in reaction, all at once.

I took a drink of water, "Say that again?"

"We've all, at the point of a very similar introduction as you're having now, agreed to take three quarters of our assets and put them in the 'community pool' so to speak, so we can pursue these projects together. In addition, we agree to diluting our remaining assets to the basic cost-of-living New York state standard, over the following five years, at a rate of an additional 10 percent until we've reached that standard."

I took another drink of water. *Had these people gone*

THE STORY OF COLE CARSON | 155

mad? I was emphatically wishing I had taken the out earlier in the conversation because I was now breaking out in a sweat, knowing there was an "opportunity" for me coming soon.

The table turned quiet. I was looking at my hands as I was ringing them. Gretta and Steve were looking at my hands as well. There was an unspoken acknowledgement that this conversation would now be invading my personal space and was revealing some very personal and vulnerable information about them as well.

"Cole, we would like you to consider joining us as a partner," Steve posed the piercing question.

"Why?" I raised my voice suddenly and harshly. I was bothered and felt impositioned. "Why would you do this to such a large degree? Can't you do this with more caution and moderation?" I heard a sense of disgust and offense in my voice, but I couldn't help myself.

They paused, and I shook my head and actually felt my teeth grinding together. "What is driving this degree of commitment? It
seems strange, or cult-like!" I said it. I was exposed. I was angry.

"Cole, it is uncomfortable, this level of commitment. I agree. And the only thing driving me, personally, is that building my own wealth became empty, and I wanted to figure out what else there was," disclosed Steve.

I looked around the pub. People were gathering, four or five to a table, laughing, having drinks, and having a really carefree, wonderful time. I was extremely envious. Two women were laughing so loud that others were looking their way. Obviously something very funny was said, one of them couldn't catch her breath. "Oh my God!" the other yelled. There was an air of careless steam being blown off from the stressful office days that had just ended.

"Cole, we need to wrap this up for tonight and here's the deal: This is a one time offer, and you have two weeks to respond. After that, the offer is off the table, and our confidentiality agreement is all that will stand in our relationship," Gretta stated flatly, seriously, and finally.

"Two weeks?" I looked back at the laughing women who were now back in conversation with one another. "Why would I do this?" I asked unbelievably.

"Yes, that's the question Cole," said Steve.

"What are you talking about, Steve? I've just met you, and you're acting like this whole thing makes sense, and I'd be a fool to pass this up!" I said angrily.

A tall, blonde waitress with too much make-up on and a low-cut blouse came to our table just then. Sensing the tension, her eyebrows raised, she quietly asked, "Can I get anyone anything else?"

"I would like a shot of whiskey," I said before thinking. "Who else will join me? My treat!" I felt a little on edge and rash. I felt like forcing my new friends, like they were forcing me.

"Sure," said Gretta. "Me too," said Steve.

"Great, let's do this," I said. Our waitress nodded, thankful to clearly know what to bring and leave.

It got really quiet then. It was awkward. Gretta appeared to be looking at a unique ring on her left hand, just next to her wedding ring. It was silver, with an amethyst stone set in the center. She twisted it right and left on her hand and then continued to rub her hand, as if it were cramping. Steve stared at the center of the table, slightly and slowly nodding, almost indistinguishably.

The waitress brought the drinks right away and set them down in front of us. I took mine and raised it to each of them. As they raised theirs, I toasted, "To you both! What the hell, for giving it all away to the poor!"

I froze.

My glass was raised and fixed in the air.

Both Gretta and Steve threw down their drinks, and I was . . . somewhere else. I was side-by-side again with Jonathan Sanders, and I heard him: "Cole, sell everything, and give it to the poor. Then, you'll be secure forever. And, start following me."

"Drink up, Cole, you have a big decision ahead of you," called out Steve, but I barely could hear him above my pulsating heart and the thumping in my ears. I set my drink down slowly. "Cole? You alright?" Steve checked.

My lips were moving, but nothing was coming out. I was staring at my drink.

"Cole?" asked Gretta.

"Okay, okay, think, think," I heard myself say. I slowly regained focus and looked up at her.

"Cole, let's finish for tonight, we understand this is a lot to consider, and you have my number. If you have any more questions or need any information let me know, and I'll make sure you have it. If we don't hear from you after two weeks from today, we'll know you've decided against it. Okay?" Gretta was trying to end our time gracefully. "Thank you for the drink."

"Nice meeting you, Cole. I'll be thinking of you as you consider this opportunity," Steve stood, and I vacantly shook their hands and watched them walk out together. Our waitress now came and cleared the table, other than my drink.

"You okay?" she asked. I gave a small, conciliatory smile. "You're going to finish your drink, right? You ordered it with such gusto. I think you needed it more than your friends, and yours is the one left untouched."

"You want it?" I offered. "I don't want it anymore."

"Wish I could, but can't while I'm working ... but, if you want to drink together later?" her voice trailed off, and my arousal was instant and unannounced. I looked at her, and she smiled dangerously.

Oh God. I've got to get out of here!

"Sorry, got to get home," I said while standing and leaving money on the table. "But, thanks," and I left.

I walked out of there, went home, and crawled into bed. I never spoke about that conversation, or that night, again, ever, with anyone.

Except for with him.

✳

It was two weeks later to the day that I ran into Jonathan Sanders as I was leaving the gym. He was walking in with a friend, and our eyes caught one another's. He excused himself and walked toward me, "Cole, how are you doing?"

I was somewhat star-struck for a moment and finally was able to say, "Jonathan! Good to see you. I'm fine, and how are you?"

"Just fine," he said with ease. He set down his bag, and his hand reached out to my shoulder and patted it with firm kindness and familiarity. He smiled and looked around a bit, then lowered his voice some. "So, what did you think of your evening recently at the Press Room?" he forged right in.

I smiled, and then nodded. "Well, that's right, you were there too, " I acted as if that had just occurred to me. "Well, it was nothing if it wasn't fascinating and quite a learning experience for me," I said, not ready for this conversation.

"I wondered what you were thinking and also what you've decided to do about the offer to become a part of Concerning New York?" He asked with such openness, that I was thrown for a minute.

"Well, I've decided to decline the offer," I gave in and said. I felt immediately sad, realizing that this would put potential distance between Jonathan and me.

"Hmm, I see," he said. Hand still on my shoulder.

"I'm very impressed by all of it, I just don't know that I can jump into something . . . so extreme," I heard apology in my voice, and felt more sadness.

"Cole, I understand. No further explanation needed. I'm still a big fan of yours," he smiled and patted my shoulder once more before bending to pick up his bag, seeming to be ready to move on.

"Jon," I grasped, "you said something to me, the first time we met, about following you. I hope I'm not in any way . . . outside of that offer by not joining the club."

"No, Cole," he smiled, "there's no club." He set his bag down once more, came back a little closer, and spoke quietly. "There's no club in following me. It's just following me, in whatever club you find yourself in, wherever your life takes you."

He pulled me in for a hug, patting my back, then holding my shoulders as he backed up and looked into my eyes, smiling warmly. Then picked up his bag once again and left.

I had no words in response. I had no idea what he meant. I only knew one thing right then: I was glad the offer still stood.

Epilogue

C hristmas that same year.

Mark DiAngelo was driving home to Connecticut to be with his family. The night before he had held a Christmas party at the community center, and had about 55 high school football players, their girlfriends, and some of their families there for a dinner, some fun gag gifts, and the sharing of the Christmas story. He was on a high as he drove home, listening to seasonal carols on the radio and singing along. His cell phone rang, and he picked up, not recognizing the number.

"Hello?"

"Hi Mark, this is Cathy, from Cole Carson's office. Happy holidays to you," she paused.

"Oh, hi Cathy. Thank you, and to you too."

"Mark, sorry to call you in the midst of the holiday, but Cole wanted me to contact you. This is a little unusual, but Cole somehow knew you were headed home to Connecticut for Christmas and asked that you make a stop on your way home."

"Yes, I told him my plans. What is this about though?"

"I don't actually know. He just asked that you get off on the Sutton Avenue exit, and pull into the McDonald's right off the freeway, and … this is going to sound funny, but he asked that you go in and order a 'Cole Carson special' whatever that is." There was amusement in her voice and maybe a hint of embarrassment.

"Well, alright, I'm about ten minutes away. Can't imagine what this is all about, but tell him I'll do it."

"Okay, Mark. And Merry Christmas to you and your family."

"And to you as well. Thank you, Cathy."

Ten minutes later, Mark pulled into a parking place and headed inside. A tall skinny kid with long blonde hair and large black-rimmed glasses asked from behind the cash register, "Can I take your order?"

"Uh, yes, I was told to order the 'Cole Carson' special?" Mark smiled and raised his eyebrows in question.

"The what?" he smiled back.

"The 'Cole Carson' special?"

"Uh, I don't know anything about that. Hold on just a minute," he left to go ask someone, maybe his manager, about it. Mark stepped aside trying to keep from holding up the line. A woman came back with him, and he pointed to Mark. Mark smiled and she smiled back.

"Here," she held out her hand. He held out his hand, and she dropped a key into it. She proceeded to tell him what he was wondering, "Look for the white van outside."

"White van?" he stared at the key.

"Yes, that's all I know. Can we get you anything else?"

she was ready to move on.

"No, thank you," he continued to stare at the key, and then he headed outside. In the back corner of the parking lot, backed into its space, was a very new looking white 15-passenger van with a note in the windshield. He walked over, used the key in the lock, hopped in, and took in the 'new car' smell. He reached for the note that simply said, "Mark."

Mark,

> *Time for some new wheels! And while we're at it, it's time for more than that. Enclosed is the name of a developer in the city who I've hired to develop a neighborhood center right next to the high school. From our foundation, we've decided to come behind your work and resource whatever you need to continue supporting and encouraging those kids. You are making a difference in their lives, and you've made a difference in mine. Thank you. And have a nice Christmas with your family!*

> *Cole Carson*

✳

Patty left the Rescue Mission after their holiday meal for the homeless, as the clouded winter sun was setting on Christmas Eve. This year they ran short on the turkey and dressing, so she did her best to fill up on potatoes, gravy, and cranberry sauce. She pulled her cart on wheels with her old pink-gloved hands, and pulled her scarf up around her cheeks as snow flurries began to fall. She had about 10 blocks to walk to the shelter. She needed to get there by 9 p.m. to make sure she'd get a bed.

She planned to go by the building on her way to the shelter to say Merry Christmas to the nighttime security guard, Howard, who often watched her stuff for her when she needed to go somewhere. He wasn't supposed to help her, but the two of them had been part of the building for several years now, and he helped her anyway. Once all the employees cleared out earlier today, he had brought a few of her bags inside, out of the cold and behind the security desk in the entry way.

As she approached the building, she saw a flicker of lights in the lobby, off to the side, over near the beautifully decorated Christmas tree. Every year, the Monday after Thanksgiving, the workers put up the magnificent tree and welcomed in the season. Lights glistened beautiful colors and often warm coffee or cider sat available during the day on a small, decorated table next to the tree, at least that is what Patty had always imagined it to be, looking in from the outside.

She walked up to the doors and noticed that the flickering lights were candles lit on a table full of place settings for a meal. She rubbed her eyes with the backs of her gloves and looked again at this setting. In all the years she had had a place outside of this building, she had never seen the lobby used for a nice meal.

Not seeing Howard anywhere, she knocked on the glass door. She had made the mistake one time long ago of entering the building, needing to use the bathroom. She remembered now with a cringe the embarrassment of two security guards calling her out of the bathroom just as she had sat down and yelling at her to get out of there then escorting her out as she was trying to pull on her coat, while trying to keep her eyes down.

She knocked again now, but no one came. She could hear some music coming from inside. She pulled her coat collar up around her neck as the snow started coming down a little harder. She saw the elevator light go on just then, announcing the arrival of a car to the lobby.

Howard must have been checking the upper floors. She was relieved to know he was coming now.

It wasn't Howard who came out of the elevator though; it was a woman, followed by two kids, followed by a man in a suit. She leaned closer to the glass. Something wasn't right. They didn't have their coats on. They weren't leaving the building.

The man in the suit was suddenly familiar; he was one of the men that passed her all the time.

Mr. Carson.

They were all dressed up and looked over at the table and the tree. As she realized that they were to have their special Christmas meal here, all to themselves, she suddenly felt fearful of being caught with her stuff kept in the lobby by Howard. She backed up quickly and tried to hide behind a planter just outside the doors. However, just as she did, she saw Mr. Carson notice her, and for a moment their eyes caught one another's.

Suddenly, the family looked away from the table and followed Mr. Carson, walking through the lobby and toward the front doors. Patty turned, quickly grabbed her cart and wheeled it around, and began leaving as fast as she could.

The door opened. "Patty, don't leave," she heard him say. She stopped, froze still. "Please come inside," he invited.

She turned slowly, "Me?"

"Yes, you Patty. Please, come inside," he said again.

"I'm not supposed to go in there, " she said.

"Patty, it's okay, we'd like to invite you in to be with us," he said.

One hour later, it was Patty's turn to descend to the lobby in the elevator, with Connie at her side. She had showered, dressed, and had her hair done, with Connie's help. The others, along with Howard, were standing at the table, waiting for them.

Patty couldn't believe her eyes. A glazed brown turkey was steaming in the middle of the table; dressing and gravy were on either side. Rolls, salads, desserts, and drinks were all set out. She had never sat at a table like this.

First slowly, then steadily, tears rolled down her cheeks,

as she sat at the place with her name on a gold and silver card.

"Mr. Carson, I don't know what this is about. Why? Why are you doing this?" she said in a very small voice, looking down at her hands in her lap.

"Cole, please call me Cole," he said as his eyes engaged hers. "Patty, I have been walking by you for six or seven years now. Today, I'm done walking by you. Today, me and my family, would like to share a meal with you, and to say 'Merry Christmas.'"

Smiles were shared, Cole reached out to hold Connie's hand as he continued, "Patty, we would like to help care for you, to help make your life less difficult and more possible."

Patty looked at each of them, not able to understand. "But, why?"

"Because we can help, Patty. And because I pass you everyday and things haven't improved for you, on your own. So, I'm wondering if we can help?" he asked.

Howard smiled at her and nodded. She smiled, and then she cried, and then she laughed. They all did. They laughed and hugged one another and toasted their drinks.

And as the meal began to be served, tears rolled down his cheeks, too. He had to use his cloth napkin to wipe tears away several times. He didn't know why exactly, except that he was overwhelmed with . . . a sense of wealth and goodness that seemed too good to be true. He couldn't make sense of it.

He didn't know he could've grown richer.

But, somehow, he had.

Thirsty

Prologue

It was during this time that political tensions were building. His popularity had grown and the current leaders were threatened by the fact that more and more people were following him. He was offering something that people hadn't known about previously. Something that gave them an opportunity to recover from the discouragement and fear they lived under. Something that gave them hope for the first time in a long while. Knowing how disruptive the efforts of his opponents could be, he decided to leave where he was staying and return to his hometown again.

This time, though, he had to go through a part of the country that he normally wouldn't travel through. The people of this particular town didn't socialize or mix with the people of his town. There he met a woman, and this is her story, which had begun years and years earlier. This is what happened there, as he was waiting outside, during that hot day when he met her, and they had a conversation.

"**M**ama, is it him, is it him?" I shouted through the crowd of thousands of people lining the streets. "Is it him, Mama? I can't see. Where is he?"

"I don't know, Mija; I can't see either," she cried out. My mother stood about a foot and a half shorter than all the others around her. Although small and weak, she lifted me up in her arms, getting me a little higher than her own eyes, "What do you see, Mija? Do you see him?"

"No Mama, not yet. I can't see anything but the flashing lights of the police cars."

We had been waiting for the Pope's visit to Mexico City for months. Iglesia de Santa Maria, our parish, had postings all throughout our neighborhood about the Holy Father's blessing to come. The preceding week had been a flurry of excitement as we all prepared ourselves to see him and to receive the magical moment of blessing.

"In our lifetimes, this may be the only time we will ever see His Holiness," said Papa over supper the night before. Aunts, uncles, cousins, and my sisters, who all filled the room, nodded in silence as we ate together. It was the awaited event of the year in the city.

Papa was what is commonly called a non-practicing Catholic. He attended mass with us at Christmas and Easter, but said he preferred his communion in the company of his own kitchen, with friends and family, enjoying wine and bread. With no father and Papa's mother dying when he was young, he was left to raise his little brother. We suspected that they were left to live on the streets for a time; however, we never discussed this with him. He didn't allow it.

The crowd was cheering and waving now, although the Pope was not in sight as of yet. We were standing shoulder to shoulder, ten rows deep of people sandwiching either side of the street. This went on for miles. Our family was scattered throughout the block here and there. My mother and I were about four rows back from the street and beginning to lack hope that we could hold our position or that my mother could hold me long enough to get a glimpse of him as he passed.

"I'm slipping Mama!" I cried, as she stumbled into a woman next to us and fell down to one knee.

Just then, a gentleman of well over six feet tall grabbed me under my arms and lifted me onto his shoulders. I cheered in delight and clapped, and I could hear my mother saying, "Gracias señor," thanking him.

"Puedes ver, Mija? Puedes ver El Papa?" He shouted to see if I could see now.

And just then, I could.

A vehicle that stood above the others was coming down

the street in the middle of the brigade. Standing on top and behind a windshield covering his whole body was the Pope himself! There was a thunderous roar coming from the crowd. The surroundings were literally vibrating from the cheers and the frantic jumping up and down all at once to get a glimpse of him.

"What do you see, Mija? What do you see?" cried my poor mother, who could only possibly see the heads and bouncing waves of outstretched hands in front of her, at best.

"I see him, Mama! I see him!" I shouted.

The Pope's parade was moving quickly. The passing was short. His Holiness, dressed all in white, held up his hand of blessing as he motioned the formation of the cross in large sweeping strokes. We reached out our hands toward him with shouts of joy as we received his blessing, the moment we had all been waiting for.

His smile was kindly fixed, his eyes focused on us with sincerity, and his hands and arms spanned the breadth of his eager crowd ensuring his extended grace to us all.

"Gracias Papa! Gracias por todo! Thank you for everything!" I shouted. Women and men alike pulled out their handkerchiefs, blotting their tears of joy and relief. The crowd continued to roar.

As he passed, people were hugging one another and holding each other. My mother was hugging the man beneath me, and I could see she was crying with joy. Children were dancing all around, as they came out of arms and off

shoulders. I heard music beginning in celebration coming
from somewhere behind me.

As I was let down, I thanked the man and hugged my
mother. "Did you receive his blessing, Mija? Did you receive
it?" she asked.

"Yes Mama, I did! I did. Did you receive it, Mama?
Did you receive it, too?" I asked her.

She smiled sadly, grabbed my hand and began to steer
me out of the crowd with a bit of a limp from her stumble and
back in the direction of our house. "I hope so, Mija . . . I hope
so."

The parties that evening were full of stories of the
Pope's visit. There were three extra masses added into the
weekend's schedule so that people could worship and give
thanks. Something new had washed over our old
neighborhood, and unexplainable hope was felt by both young
and old, many of whom hadn't known hope in years.
Whether real or imagined, we all celebrated the blessing he
had come to deliver and enjoyed the hope that maybe life
would be better now.

※

It was two years later, and I was preparing for my First
Communion. Our class of 23 eight year olds had been
meeting every Wednesday for the last year, and now it was
our turn to confirm our faith and commitment to the church.

Each week we would be given a lesson, and then memorize
our prayers. Padre Raul arrived each time, carrying books, a
couple of relics that we would be learning about, and a bag
with crackers and juice to help the roomful of us get through
the 60 minute class. The room always smelled of ammonia
and incense blended together, and it was usually about 15
minutes after arriving before the smell disappeared.

It was hard to tell if Padre Raul wanted to be there or,
as was more likely, forced to teach our class. He often came in
ruffled and unprepared and always seemed frustrated by our
lack of attention. About half way through the lesson, he
would often abandon the teaching, pull out the snacks, and tell
everyone it was free time. This was our favorite part.

As the time came for our First Communion service, I
had already selected my dress, shoes, hat, and purse that I
would carry. Mama had been planning the food for the after-
party for the last two weeks. She had made the tamales ahead
of time with several neighborhood women, many of whose
children were also being confirmed that day. There had been
a full kitchen of good smells for days in preparation for this
celebration.

Mama worked around the house tirelessly. She was
always cooking the next meal, and doing laundry. She was
very quiet, and often held a sad expression on her face,
seeming to be thinking of something a long way off. She
always tended to me, and my two older sisters and scrutinized
our appearance whenever we left the house. She was very

proud of her daughters, and whenever we overheard conversation between her and the neighborhood women, it was often about us and our accomplishments.

As I was dressing for the service that day and getting ready, I could hear my parents in the back room, and their voices were unusual. I walked to the door of my bedroom that I shared with my sisters and listened. Then I pressed my ear to the door. They were arguing. His voice was beginning to rise and shout. I quickly tried to open the door, but my older sister's hand grabbed my shoulder and pulled me back.

"No Celeste, don't go to them," she said. Her eyes and face were stern.

The shouting was increasing. "But, Maria, why is he talking to her like that?" I pressed. The harshness of their tone was feeling urgent and out of control to me, as well as the concerned expression on Maria's face.

Maria was seven years older than me. As long as I can remember, she was taking care of me, and my sister, Olivia, who we called "Livy." Livy was only two years older than me, so it was Maria who kept us in line.

Maria was a simple girl and quiet. For being 15 years old, she dressed plainly, and modestly, not paying much attention to her appearance. She was pretty, however, but in a very subdued way: large brown eyes, fair complexion, straight long hair, and a delicate smile, not often seen. She had a few friends who were much like her, and none of them seemed interested in boys, dates, or parties. They were focused on school and responsibilities.

She was very conscientious and seemed to have a different relationship with Mama than Livy and I did. She looked out for Mama, and often asked how she was doing or if she needed help.

"No!" we heard Mama scream. Something hit the wall in between our rooms and broke. Papa was yelling terrible things at her, calling her names that I had never heard before in my home. It sounded like she was running, and a door was sliding ... the closet door. Then, we heard another loud crash of something hitting a wall or door. It sounded like wood breaking into pieces.

And then, silence. Terrible silence.

We couldn't hear her now. My sister pushed passed me, and ran to their door. "Papa is everything ok?" she asked in a controlled voice. "Mama? Are you ok?"

Livy had just walked in the front door from a friend's house and was immediately aware that something was wrong. Maria was knocking softly, but persistently, at their door. Livy quickly came to me, and we continued to watch through the crack in the door. I must have been crying because I remember Livy whispering in my ear, "Shhh, Celeste, don't let him hear you."

Then, their door flew open, and the first thing I saw was the rage in my dad's eyes. He took my sister's shoulders into his hands and shook her. I thought he was hurting her. Livy and I held each other.

"Your mother is a bitch! She doesn't respect me at all! She did this to herself!" he yelled, as he threw Maria down to the ground and walked passed our door. We withdrew quickly, hoping he wouldn't see us.

He stormed out the front door, breathing heavily and swearing under his breath. We quickly went to Maria who was getting up, saying, "It's ok, I'm ok Celeste . . . let's get to Mama." Her lip was bleeding a bit, but she was wiping it away with her forearm, as she staggered to her feet.

We walked into their room and first saw the blood on the far wall, near the small closet. She was lying on the ground halfway inside. It looked like she was trying to get in, when she was struck by what used to be their nightstand.

She was unconscious. I began to scream and call out for help. Maria quietly went to her, "Mama, wake up. It's me. You're okay. Wake up Mama. He's gone now. He's done for now. Wake up Mama," as tears rolled down her cheeks. She was softly patting her limp hand, one-two-three-pause, one-two-three-pause, over and over.

"What can I do?" I was terrified and screaming. "We need to call Tio! We need to get a doctor!" I was frantic and jiggling Mama's leg, trying to get her to wake up. "Mama! Mama, open your eyes!"

Maria's ear was to Mama's mouth, watching her chest. "She's breathing." Mama let out a low moan and turned her head a little.

"Get her some water," Livy said, standing behind me

and looking at me with a sad face. "She'll need some water; you go and get her that." Her tone and her face betrayed that she knew about this, like Maria.

I ran to the kitchen. The water bottle near the sink was nearly empty and only offered drips to the glass, as I shook it and slapped the end of it, desperately willing more water to come out. I ran to the back door, opened it, and looked around for any discarded used bottles and found one with a little more water. Again, I pounded those few swallows into the glass for Mama, driven to bring her something, anything, that would help her.

When I rounded the corner to her room, Mama's one, unswollen eye saw me coming, and then filled with tears. "No, Celeste, don't look at me," she cried out. Maria said, "Celeste, leave the water here, it will help Mama. Go to your room and get ready."

Somehow, I was making Mama worse. I didn't understand. I set down the glass, turned to leave as tears now filled my eyes. I could hear Mama sob and say, "I'm so sorry Celeste, lo siento mucho mija."

Our bedroom was just as it was before this started. My dress was laid out on the bed, and my shoes on the floor below. Everything seemed the same. However, life had changed and gotten much worse in those moments.

Mama didn't make it to my First Communion that day, nor did Papa. My sisters helped Mama get into bed and then cleaned and bandaged her cuts. I peeked in from the door every few minutes. One eye remained swollen shut, as she wincingly held a bag of ice on it. Her lip was cut badly. She didn't say anything. My sister Maria did all the talking, while picking up the dreadful pieces of our family's secret. "We'll take care of Celeste, Mama, and get her to First Communion. Don't worry," she was softly assuring.

Once my mother was taken care of, my sisters and I finished getting ready and walked to the church, looking perfect head to toe. We smiled politely, participated in the ceremony, and secured my confirmation to the church, all on our own.

"We must hold our heads high and not say a word about this to anyone. Do you understand, Celeste? Especially not the family, not a word!" Maria had said. Her face was stern and her eyes were staring straight ahead. Livy walked with her eyes downcast and was very quiet.

First Communion didn't seem that important anymore. *Why would he hurt her like this? Why did she let him? Why didn't she, or my sisters, do something about this?*

As much as these questions were pressing me, I was also aware of my fear of him, more than anyone I'd ever known, and this seemed to quiet these questions. We wouldn't do anything or say anything because he frightened her, he frightened my sisters, and now, he frightened me.

The party that was to happen after my First Communion was quickly switched to my Tia Colette's house. There were plenty of smiles, music, and more tamales than we could eat, yet no one said a word about the absence of my parents.

✳

For the next couple of years, this story repeated itself over and over again, as we each perfected our roles with practice, much like theater rehearsals. I had my duties down of getting water and bandages. My mother grew to accept me knowing the real situation, and seemed comforted by my singing of some of the songs I learned in mass. This was also part of my role. Her favorite was "Dios es Mi Refugio," God is My Refuge, which I must've sung a hundred times over those years.

Livy questioned Maria about our need to be so discreet, but in the end, Maria persuaded us to keep quiet, and to try and protect Mama.

My relationship with my dad consisted of quietly listening whenever he was around. I never wanted to cause a problem for fear that he would become angry. He worked, came home, ate, drank too much, and then went to bed. That was dad's role and we always felt relieved when he accomplished another day, was in bed, and we could all breath a sigh of relief. The only laughter in our house, was after he passed out, when we would each try to cheer up Mama and be glad if she smiled.

✳

When I began my second year of *preparatoria*, or high
school, there was a boy named Jose who began to ask about
me through my friends and began talking to me at school. He
was the first boy I remember liking. He was very good
looking and made people laugh all the time. He worked at the
market, boxing groceries on the weekends. He lived a few
blocks from our house and began to walk me home after
school as the weeks went on.

I thought he was spending time with me to get to know
Livy, who was very popular and very pretty. I was rather
awkward still and had never received much attention from
boys. Still, I enjoyed Jose's company and we laughed a lot,
even if his interest was in Livy.

One day, though, as we reached my house on the walk
home, Jose was standing closer to me than usual. Without
saying anything, he reached behind my waist and pulled me
slowly to him, and began kissing me. I was tense and afraid
and pulled back. But, he just looked at me and smiled and
pulled me close and began kissing me again.

As I went along with him, I began to enjoy it. I enjoyed
his embrace and his kiss, and most of all I enjoyed that he
wanted me. When we finished, I was dizzy. He left quickly
when Mama walked out our front door, giving us a look of
worry and disapproval.

"Mija, come here!" she said.

I walked over, glancing at Jose as he walked away. "Yes

Mama?" I asked, wiping my mouth and feeling its smile.

"Celeste, don't get mixed up with boys, you'll lose your direction," was what she said, rather sharply. "Celeste? Did you hear me?"

"Yes, Mama, yes I heard you. He kissed me Mama, he likes me," I was nearly singing. I couldn't help it. I hadn't ever had anyone express desire for me before, like that, and I was lightheaded and . . . lifted somehow. For the first time, I was untethered from sadness and was floating out and away from it.

"Sure he does, Celeste, he wants something you don't want to give," she cynically frowned. Her disapproving voice quickly snared the string of the kite I'd become.

In all the days, months, and years now, that I had spent feeling sorry and protective of Mama, suddenly I felt angry with her *Why wasn't she happy for me? A boy liked me! Other than Papa, and my cousins, no boy had ever talked to me, or ever acted interested.*

"Mama, I've just kissed him, that's all," I looked down and began to walk around her.

"Mija, that's how it all begins," she warned, and picked up her broom and began to sweep the porch. That night, after dinner, I quickly finished the dishes and went to my room.

A while later, I heard Papa call out, "Celeste! Ven aqui! Come here!" His voice had a startling edge. *Mama wouldn't say anything to him, would she? She knows he can't be trusted.*

When I got to the family room, the TV was off, and

Mama was standing behind his chair where he was sitting and looking down. My stomach sank.

"Yes, Papa?" my voice quivered.

"Mama tells me that a boy is walking you home?" he said with a frown.

"Y-y-yes, Papa," I said quietly.

"Celeste, boys who go after girls are up to no good. I will not have my daughters having babies before they are married," he blurted.

"Ramon!" Mama raised her voice. I saw a quick flash of apology to me in her face, but it was too late.

"Silencio!" he shouted. "I am the man of the house, and I can say what I want to say. Celeste, do you hear me?" His eyes were bloodshot; he'd already been drinking. The last thing I wanted was for him to hurt us again.

"Yes, Papa," I cowered.

"Now, go, and remember that you are not to disgrace our family!"

"Yes, Papa," I looked down, and then quickly left the room.

※

Despite this warning from Papa, Jose walked me home everyday after that, and everyday we would kiss as we parted. We began to kiss out of eyesight of my house and Mama, and then out of eyesight of everyone. Although I knew that Papa

wouldn't want me to do this, I couldn't seem to resist Jose's
affections.

There was a side yard to the house next door that was
surrounded by tall hedges. One day, Jose pulled me in that
yard, as we laughed at one of his jokes, and he began to kiss
me. At first it was our normal kiss and embrace, but then he
grew more aggressive, and I surprised myself that I responded
in the same way.

I was losing my breath and control, when his hands
were quickly without restraint and underneath my clothes,
pulling them off. I pulled back, and looked him in the eye,
"Wait Jose, wait," I was breathless. He quickly kissed me
again, building momentum.

"Jose, please, wait . . . " I pushed at his shoulders. But he
didn't stop. Instead his strength overpowered me, and he held
me tight as he took me down to the ground. I began to feel
afraid. "No, Jose, we can't," I cried.

Just then, I could hear Mama's screen door on the other
side of the house, and I could hear her call, "Celeste!" Jose's
hand covered my mouth, and I didn't know what to do. I
couldn't have Mama see us this way. I was half naked by now.
Jose was not stopping, and I knew that I could not call for
help. He smiled, and he knew it too.

I was trapped.

As Jose continued, I was sinking in the powerlessness of
my silence. He was forceful and determined. Something
inside me grew very quiet and died, and I just gave in, waiting

for it to be over, so I could get away.

After we were finished, he got up and combed his hair, while my clothes were all strewn about. "Would you hand me my shirt?" I asked him. It was flung onto a bush just behind him. He glanced at it, grabbed it, and tossed it to the ground to my right, just out of reach. Covering myself with my hands and arms, I got up and reached for my shirt, turned away from him and put it on quickly. When I turned back around, he had walked out of the side yard. When I walked out, he was talking with a boy who was walking by. I heard him say my name, and they laughed.

I wanted to scream at him. I felt a flush of anger and pain ripple through me, as I began to run to my house. He quickly stopped me, grabbing my arm as I passed.

"Celeste, don't run. People will notice us," he cautioned.

We walked together to my house, and fortunately, Mama had gone inside. Jose gave me a short, forceful kiss on the cheek, and I ran up to the house and to my room. I silently cried, holding my face in my pillow, not wanting anyone to hear. When I heard my sister Maria arrive home, I quickly went to the bathroom to clean up and change clothes since mine were now stained.

Later that night, after Papa had fallen asleep, I walked those clothes out to the burn pile and buried them. If I could've lit them on fire and burned them without people noticing, I would have right then and there.

❋

Even though I was left feeling terrible after those moments with Jose, we continued to see each other. It seems like every morning I would wake up, deciding to avoid him and determined to stay with my friends, but by the time I would see him at school, I would crave his attention and not want anyone else to have it.

After a few more times on the side yard after school, I began to give in more and more easily. The longer we continued to see each other, the more and more his attentions felt like love, even if it was still somewhat forceful.

After the holidays that year, I was at the market with a friend, and afterwards, we were waiting out in front for the bus. As we were talking, my friend caught site of something, then quickly looked away and stumbled over her words so noticeably that I asked her what was wrong. "Nothing, nothing," she was looking down at her feet.

Not believing, I retraced her gaze and saw Jose in the alley across the street, with his hands all over a girl, with the pursuit that I recognized.

"Celeste," she said, "Let's go. He's a jerk, Celeste, let's go."

I couldn't pull my eyes away. I couldn't believe it. I felt so foolish and stupid. I couldn't move.

"What?" I turned to her, "Yeah, let's go." Eyes stinging, we walked the opposite way to the next bus stop on the line that would take us home.

I never cried about Jose. In fact, although it was terrible to see him with another girl, I somehow expected it. I knew that I wasn't anything special. I saw him at school the next Monday and avoided him until he finally grabbed me in the hall and asked what was going on. Without thinking, I told him that I was sleeping with another guy at school, and that I didn't want anything to do with him anymore.

The deserved hurt that I saw in his eyes felt soothing, and made me feel strong, like maybe I had won. However, that didn't last long. As I walked away I said to myself, *I'm done with boys.*

※

Later that month, we were having dinner at the table when Papa announced that we were moving to Los Angeles, California. We were completely silent. We'd never known anyone who moved away. Los Angeles felt like another world to us.

"Why, Papa?" asked Maria, who was nearly finished with her college degree and about to receive her *licenciatura.*

"I'm tired of this life here, there is no opportunity, always the same, every day, every year," he took a drink and wiped his mouth. "I will find better work there, and you and your mother can work, too, and the younger girls will have better schools to go to," he finished.

"I like my school," Livy said softly, looking down.

"Silencio Olivia!" he raised his voice. "I know this is a surprise to you, but you will see that you'll like it there," he spoke, while nodding in agreement with himself.

Mama was silent, and only looked at her plate, picking at the food. I didn't know whether to be happy or sad. I felt a little of both. Los Angeles was the same as Disneyland to me, both fantasy and fairytale all mixed into one. But, what about our family here? What about my friends?

"We will leave next month," he announced.

Six weeks later, we were unpacking boxes in our two-bedroom apartment in Southeast Los Angeles. The move had been difficult to say the least. Our family in Mexico couldn't believe it at first, and tried to convince my father otherwise, but eventually took his stubborn and unrelenting decision as final.

It was perhaps the hardest on my mother's family. By now I had learned that they were all aware of how Papa treated Mama, and they feared her moving further away from them and from help when she needed it.

My mother never caved in to their sadness, though. Instead she adopted this quiet, detached resolve about what her future might hold.

Papa sold our small house, and much of what we owned, and used this money for our plane tickets and beginning our life in Los Estados Unidos.

I hated to leave, but there were many things about life

there that I hated as well. I had come to hope that by moving and starting "in the land of Disney" that perhaps our story could change, that Papa would change, or that maybe Mama would have some fight in her.

The plane ride alone seemed to confirm our hope for change and adventure. My sisters and I squealed with delight, as we all peered out the window and watched Mexico become smaller and smaller underneath us, and then fade away.

✳

Beginning school in LA was hard and scary for each of us. Maria began classes at the city college and began cleaning houses in the evenings with Mama. Mama walked Livy and I to our first day of high school about seven blocks away. The neighborhood had a lot of graffiti on the walls of the buildings and on some of the houses. As we walked up to the office, the groups of students around the door were smoking and looking at us with disapproval.

"Look who's here? The sister saints," said one girl, wearing all black, and lots of make-up. The group laughed.

"Look ahead, Celeste," whispered Livy. I felt frightened.

After two weeks of walking alone to school, eating alone at lunch, and talking to no one but each other, a boy came up to us one day as we were leaving school. His name was Felipe. He was friendly and had an amazing smile. We had seen him with the groups who had been mean to us.

"Can I walk you home?" he asked me.

"Sure," I looked at Livy and walked over next to him
and in front of her. She frowned but stayed quiet. He asked
about our move to LA and what life was like in Mexico, he
seemed interested in getting to know us.

"So, what was the name of the boyfriend you left
behind?" he smiled at me. Livy looked down, again staying
quiet.

"Jose" I lied. I liked him thinking that I did leave a
boyfriend behind for some reason. Felipe suddenly slipped his
fingers into mine and held my hand as we began to walk
again.

"Well, he's a long way away now," he smiled. I began to
feel really excited again.

As we approached our apartment, Livy said while
tugging at my sleeve, "Let's go Celeste, here's our place."

I looked at Felipe, and back at her, "You go on ahead
inside, I'll be right in." She frowned, but let go and walked in.
I turned back to Felipe to be met with his warm lips all around
mine, pulling me close to him from my waist. I was falling,
drifting again, and slipping into a dream.

We went on for some time, his hands all over my back,
then he pulled back, "See you tomorrow," he smiled and said.

"Mija! Time to come in!" yelled Mama with alarm. I
watched him leave, and somehow knew that this would be
different this time.

✳

It turned out that Felipe only lived two blocks away in another apartment. Over the next several weeks, sometimes he would walk us to our place, and a few times I walked him further down to his. We quickly became a couple at school, which really helped change the social scene for Livy and me. He introduced us to all of his friends, and they became our friends. Well, I should say, my friends. Livy made other friends with some smart kids from her classes. We were finding different groups.

When I began to come home later and later after school, Livy pulled me aside one day into the bathroom and closed the door.

"What are you doing, Celeste?" she whispered close to my face.

"What do you mean?" I said.

"I hear you are sleeping with Felipe now. Mija, you are getting yourself into trouble!" she warned.

"I haven't slept with Felipe! Who told you that?" I countered.

"Shhh, Mama will hear you!" she covered. "It doesn't matter who told me, people all know. He's told his friends," she revealed. "You are getting a reputation, Celeste, and a bad one."

"What's so bad about that?" I carelessly laughed with a sneering smile, trying to cover the confusion I felt inside.

"Watch yourself, Celeste," she warned.

And, I guess I did. I tried to be discreet about our afternoons together.

Until, I skipped a period.

After a week, I began to panic.

I decided to tell Livy and asked her what I should do. I wanted to believe it wasn't true. I was so afraid of Papa. Livy talked me into doing a pregnancy test and went with me to get one at the store and stayed with me until I read the result.

Positive.

"Oh dear God. What am I going to do?" I cried to her.

"Shhh, Celeste," she put her arms around me. "You have some choices," she continued. We sat and cried for awhile, then she said, "You can have the baby, and give it away if you need to," she sadly smiled, "or . . . "

"Or what, have an abortion? I can't do that, Livy," I cried. I could not disgrace my family. I could not humiliate Mama and Papa. *What would Papa do?*

I walked to Felipe's that evening and asked him to meet me outside. "Felipe, I'm late," I blurted out, as he was trying to kiss me. He stopped.

"What do you mean?" he asked.

"It's what you think I mean," I stepped back, looking at the sidewalk below.

He said nothing and looked down. After moments passed with nothing said, I finally continued, "I'm pregnant, Felipe."

He turned away from me, and walked with his hands on his head, "No!" he hissed. Then turned back at me and shouted, with anger written all over his face, "No!"

Whatever I expected, I didn't expect this. I took more steps back, "What?" I couldn't believe his reaction. "'No,' what?"

"No, Celeste, no. Get rid of it!" he walked close to me now and was whispering, "There can't be a baby."

"But," I stammered, "But, wait, that's it? Is that all you have to say?" I still couldn't believe it.

"You heard me, Celeste. Do what you have to do. There is no baby."

At this, he ran into his apartment and left me standing there alone. Alone. It was instantly clear. This was my problem, and I must deal with it, alone.

✳

One of Livy's new friends had a friend who had had an abortion. She had dropped out of school shortly after, and I wanted to talk with her. So, one evening after dinner, I walked over to her apartment building, telling Mama that I had to go to do homework at a friend's house.

Jessica answered the door and stepped out onto the porch with me. "What is it?" she asked.

"I'm pregnant," I decided to come out with it straight. I was desperate, and felt that she would understand this and that we could get right to the point of my visit.

Her eyebrows arched, "Oh?" she said.

"Yes, and I'm afraid," was all I could say.

Then, she recoiled coolly. "Are you wondering about my abortion?" she asked, suddenly understanding the reason for my visit.

"Yes," I confessed.

"Well, I had one. It was horrible. And I don't want to talk about it now, other than to tell you that I went to the clinic at the Med Center, and it all happened in about 30 minutes, and it was over" she was looking down.

"How are you now? Why aren't you in school?" I pressed. I had to know.

"I'm fine. I just didn't want to be around anyone after that. I do independent studies now," she finished. "I've got to go now. Good luck." She went quickly inside and shut the door between us, ending any further information I was hoping to get from her.

Fearing the sadness I sensed in Jessica, and at the same time, the beatings that either I, or Mama, would likely endure from Papa, I decided that I could live with the sadness better.

Livy and I went to the clinic the following Friday after school, so that I could have time to rest if needed over the weekend. I filled out the forms, went into the office, and walked out 30 minutes later, as Jessica had said, with my history of Felipe and the pregnancy erased.

As I left the clinic, I passed a girl about my age walking

in. She was clutching her oversized purse, and her mascara was smeared under her red and watering eyes. She was skinny, and her shoulders were curled over, in a large, blue flannel shirt.

Poor girl . . . was all I could think.

＊

Although Mama and we girls had continued all along, over the years, to attend mass each week, I had avoided confession since I began to be involved with Jose. It was too much to face, and I decided that mass was good enough for me.

However, with the abortion now some months behind me, I was feeling an intense need to face confession. The thought of it made me become nauseous and faint. But I began to have terrible nightmares that left me feeling haunted by something inside that I couldn't get away from. I needed to be rid of the feelings I was having. I was becoming depressed and desperate. I was feeling just like Jessica had said: I didn't want to be around anyone anymore.

I considered going to confession for several weeks before I could get the courage to step inside the church one Saturday afternoon.

I sat down in a pew next to the confessional. Although it was quiet inside the church, sounds of footsteps, a door opening, a sneeze, and a cough all echoed loudly in the somewhat hollow building with tiled floors. The light was dimly coming through a stained glass window of Jesus on the cross. As I looked up at the window, I was comforted by the memory of Padre Raul years ago teaching all of us about God and the church. It was cold inside the church, and I gathered my sweater around myself as I crossed my arms around my stomach to keep warm.

There was a stream of random confessors that came in and out, all looking quite matter-of-fact, and business-as-usual. They neither looked worried nor relieved, and I wondered what I would feel like once I was finished.

I sat there wondering if I could do this. *How long had it been since the day I had received the Holy Father's blessing? Where was that blessing now? Have I sinned too badly that it is forever gone?*

Just then the burgundy curtain opened up, and I thought I heard a voice say, "Next?" It startled me and, without thinking, I moved inside and closed the curtain behind me.

Some moments passed, as I saw the Father's silhouette looking downward through the screen. "In the name of the Father, and of the Son, and of the Holy Spirit. My last confession was, was, uh, many years ago," I began as I had learned years ago.

"'For this is My blood of the covenant, which is poured out for many for forgiveness of sins,' sayeth the Lord," he quoted to me.

"Father, I have disobeyed my parents," I said out of habit from when I last came.

"Daughter, as penance, say three Hail Mary prayers each day for the next week," he paused, "Anything else?"

I coughed and cleared my throat. Sweating and feeling my breath become really shallow, I whispered, "Uh . . . uh, I have been wrongly with a boy," was all I could get out. My heartbeat was loud in my ears, and I wondered if he heard me.

"Have you had intercourse then?" he openly asked, quieting his voice as well. I could see his silhouette look up behind the screen. His hair was wavy; his nose was large and bold. He then looked straight ahead to the side, seemingly at nothing. I took a deep breath, trying to hold off the lightheadedness.

"Uh . . . Yes, Father," I cringed with embarrassment.

"Rightly so you confess. As penance, respect the body God has given you and save yourself for marriage from here forward. Also, repeat the rosary each day for a month," he concluded. "Peace be with you child," his voice added sincerely.

"I am sorry for these and all the sins of my past life," I threw in for the finish; however, I knew I wasn't done yet. I leaned forward and put my head in my hands. It grew very quiet.

"Father, I have had an abortion," I quickly said before I might change my mind. Nausea swept over me, and I was clasping my two hands together so tightly that my knuckles were white, trying to keep them from shaking.

There was silence. He cleared his throat and said, "Oh, I see."

"Please, forgive me Father," I found myself pleading, my breathing shallow again. I tried hard not to, but I began to cry. "I'm so sorry, I just didn't know what to do," I was beginning to gasp and sniff and trying to hold it in, not wanting those outside the curtain to hear.

The silence continued.

Then he began, "There, there child. Try to calm yourself." His voice sounded hesitant, and conciliatory somehow. "How old were you and did you know that it was a mortal sin?" he asked.

"I was 17, and I guess I knew it. I felt badly, but I was afraid," I worriedly recalled. The priest nodded in the light, looking down.

He then took a deep breath of his own and began, "Child, there are some things only the Lord Himself can bring relief for, and this is one of those things. Abortion is a mortal sin and very serious. You have taken the life of a child, instead of facing the consequences of your actions. This is out of my hands," he stated apologetically, while wiping his brow with the back of his hand.

"What? I can't receive forgiveness, even though I'm confessing?" I felt more tears coming.

"No, child, forgiveness is possible, but excommunication for a time and abstaining from Holy

Communion is required," he explained.

"Excommunication? What does that mean? And what about forgiveness?" I panicked.

"Well, it means you are to be excluded from the church community for a time," he said.

"You can't do that, can you?" I pleaded again. "Please," I was desperate. He shook his head slowly side to side as his silhouette now looked down and away from me.

I was confused. *Excluded ... from the community.*

I threw open the drape and saw two women waiting in line, both looking at me with alarm. *Had they heard? Or were they noticing my tears?* As I stepped out of the confessional, my heel caught itself, and I tripped and went down to my knees and hands. A moan of weeping slipped out of me. I quickly drew in a sharp breath and held it in.

I got up and back to my feet, keeping my eyes down, and walked as fast as I could beyond the women. As I turned down the main aisle, I began to run. Although my shoes were loudly drumming through the sanctuary, and I began to hear my sobbing bellow out loud, I didn't care anymore. I hated being there. I longed for some fresh air on the outside ... where I belonged.

That was the last time I went to church. That was the last year that I was in school. That was the last time I had an abortion. That was the last year I lived with my family.

✳

Six years passed, and I had received my certificate from beauty school and was working in a salon. I was setting the curl of one of my elderly clients, who held a weekly appointment - every Thursday at 11 a.m. Diana liked to talk about her children, and her grandchildren, their birthdays and holidays together, their marriages, their divorces, and their occasional funerals, all while I washed, set, dried, and styled her blueing hair.

She knew very little about me, because she liked to talk so much, and I liked to listen. It was a welcomed distraction. I had been working at this salon for nearly eight months now and, for the first time, was developing some rapport with the other stylists and clients. This was the longest job I'd held.

One day, I received a call from the day care where my four-year-old daughter, Bella, spent her days while I worked. "Celeste," said Lita, who was the woman in charge there and had become my partner in parenting, "we have a problem." Lita always sounded tired.

"What is it? Is it Bella?" I asked, trying to balance the phone while wrapping the last curling rod before I put Diana under the dryer.

"No, she's not sick, but there's someone here for her," she paused and cleared her throat a little, "someone saying that he's her father and wants to take her."

I dropped the rod on the floor and asked Diana if she would excuse me a minute. She obliged, and I walked to the back phone of the shop to continue the call.

"I don't understand, Ricky is at work and wouldn't come for her at this time of day," I concluded.

"No, it's not Ricky ... I know Ricky. This person says his name is George, and that he is Bella's father," again, a pause.

George ... George ... who is George? I panicked. I knew a George long ago, who I had met several times after we got off work for drinks. He was a decent man as I recalled, but how could he assume Bella was his?

"No, Ricky is Bella's father, you know that. He's on your parent forms, and all of his information is on that. You tell this . . . George, that he can not take her," I urged.

"I've told him that he can not take her without a signed release," she replied.

"And?"

"He said that he is her father and that he should be on the form. Celeste, you need to come down here, I can't handle this and take care of the children. I will ask him to wait outside for you," she said.

I looked at Diana, who now was getting her last rod set by another beautician in the shop.

"OK, I'll be right there," I conceded.

✳

"George?" I came around the corner and saw him leaning against the entrance of the building, looking down the street in the opposite direction, and smoking a cigarette.

"Celeste," he was walking toward me now.

"George, what are you doing here?" I said and abruptly stopped before reaching him.

"Good to see you, too," he said, as he stepped out the cigarette on the sidewalk. "Look, sorry to show up without calling, but . . . "

"Wait, George, what is going on? Is it true that you are honestly thinking that my daughter is yours?" I charged.

"Yes. The timing fits with Bella. You remember . . . "

"Wait, George, how do you know her name?" I held my palm up to him, alarmed at him calling Bella by her name.

"I learned it from the lady at the front desk," he replied and continued. "You remember when we were together. I realize it may not have been that big of a deal to you, but we did have some weeks together, and Bella's age makes it possible that I'm the father," he explained.

"Why now, George? Where have you been up until now?" I pushed.

"It would have been nice to have known about Bella, Celeste. You could've let me know. I had no idea until I saw you, and Bella, at the park on the other side of town about a month ago. I watched you for a while. She's beautiful, Celeste. She has your smile and my eyes, I think," he smiled.

Without thinking, I threw out the blow, "You weren't the only one, George." I looked down to avoid his reaction.

"Do you think you were the only one I slept with?" I asked.

He was quiet and looked down. "I'm sure I wasn't, but her age, and her birth date? The public hospital records gave the date of April 8, 1986, matching our time together perfectly," he tried.

"No, I mean you weren't the only one that month is what I'm saying," seeming to relish somehow in the delivery of the news.

"Then, I want a paternity test taken," he continued.

"Oh God, George, don't you hear what I'm saying? What we had was nothing. Bella has a dad now, and this won't help her."

"But, the woman inside said that she's never seen this 'Ricky,' or doesn't think that he lives with you. What's the story Celeste?" he asked.

"The story? The story is that there won't be a paternity test. Bella and I are fine." I turned to walk away, not sure what else to do.

"This isn't over, Celeste. If she's mine, I want to know," he called out.

Weeks later, after persistently asking for the test, George got the news he was searching for, although it wasn't what he had hoped. He wasn't the father.

※

Five years later ...

I had overslept, again, and soon realized that I wasn't

the only one. The man next to me was breathing deeply, smelled of sour wine, and had his arm laying heavy and sweaty on my stomach. As my vision moved into focus, I saw that I was staring at a glass of water on the nightstand next to the bed. I felt so dehydrated and reached over to take a sip, but just before tipping the glass, I noticed a bug floating on the surface. I was so thirsty, that I reached in, took the bug out of the glass, and took a drink anyway. It was warm and filmy, and I drank every drop. It would have to do.

The only thought I had was that I wished we had kept the window open so there would be some air.

I lifted his arm off of me and slid out from the covers and off the bed. I gathered my clothes, found my glasses, and headed for the bathroom. He stirred and sleepily called out, "Simone, where are you going?"

"It's Celeste, you fool" I said and closed the door behind me.

The mirror was cracked on the right side, but there was plenty of room to catch my reflection, and it was startling. I looked about the same as I remembered from the night before, only about 20 years older. *What a pathetic mess,* I thought, as I began the water for a hot shower.

I rubbed my face, half stretching. *How many times could a person wake up like this?*

Fifteen minutes later, as I grabbed my purse and headed out the door, I looked back to see my . . . partner . . . roll over and put the pillow over his head. "Adios," I whispered and got out of there as quickly as I could.

I was living in the lower side of South Central LA, and it was summertime. We were having a record setting heat-wave, and I knew that I only had a couple of hours to get some things done before the worst heat would arrive, and I wouldn't be able to complete my errands.

I headed toward El Mercado and began my shopping. My coupons from the state would get me about half of what I would need to feed my three children at home. Fortunately, Bella, now age 9, could watch the younger ones when I was out all night like this and would get them to day-care and school. I was working on a new excuse in my mind, because lately Bella wasn't taking my stories, I could see it in her face.

I headed down San Pedro Street and purchased bread, cereal, and cheese at the neighborhood co-op and then stopped in a cashier's shop to cash my unemployment check for this month. As I left, I caught a glimpse out of the corner of my eye of a familiar face. *Oh God,* I thought. *It can't be.* But it was. It was one of my ex-husbands, standing at the newspaper stand across the street. I tried to go unnoticed, but he looked up just in time to meet my eye.

His face held not a trace of kindness. Instead his chin rose above his shoulders, and he shook his head side-to-side in disgust. My jaw clenched, I swallowed hard, as I felt the burn in my eyes of the tears coming. I quickly looked away and walked as fast as I could away from there.

It had been two years since I had seen him. The parting

had been horrible. I could still see the anger in his face. He had wanted to hit me then, I could see it. I had been hit plenty before and was actually expecting it. However, this time, I was pushed out the door and told never to come back. I had slept with his business partner, and he had found us at our house.

I understood his anger. I didn't know why I had done it. I wasn't attracted to his partner. I didn't love him. In fact, that was the best marriage I had ever had. I still didn't know why I threw it away.

Life had become difficult over the years for my kids and me. I worked short jobs here and there, but I couldn't pay the rent or the bills or keep food in the house on my own. So, I just pieced it together, everyday of my life, one day at a time, hoping for a break.

"Celeste!" a familiar voice, and a welcomed distraction, called from the shop up ahead.

✳

In another part of the city, music blared along with the air conditioning of a packed Suburban heading southbound on Highway 101. "Get off on East 1st Street," he told his friend.

"Oh? I thought we were heading to the service in Tustin," he replied.

"First, I need to make a stop for a few things," he kept his gaze forward and pensive. They were used to plans changing and had become accustomed to asking fewer questions along the way. He took the exit and asked, "Which way?"

"Left," he replied. And this is how it usually was, not a clear destination or objective announced, but more of a turn-by-turn, step-by-step instruction. "Stay on this for a mile and a half, and take a right on South Soto," he continued.

He was sitting in the middle row of the car, on the right side near the door, with all of them squished into every seat. Someone's playlist was on and some were singing along or tapping to the music, while others were in their heads somewhere looking out and around as they drove.

He had no map, or GPS, and had made no mention of this stop when they set out earlier in the morning. It was nearing the heat of the day, and Los Angeles had been producing concerning levels of heat for the last two days, with expectations that today would land it's highest numbers yet.

They traveled without questions or comments about their direction or what the stop would be about, however, the back row whisperers were making their best guesses. They approached South Soto and had the turn signal on when he suddenly spoke out again, "I'm sorry, it's a left here. Can you make it?"

The driver quickly changed lanes and caught his eyes in the rear view mirror, which were appreciative and smiling. The driver smiled back and nodded with familiar amusement.

Soto Street soon led them into a rough looking

neighborhood. The graffiti on the buildings, and even on the houses, increased with every block. The Suburban got quiet as they all took in their surroundings.

"Where to Boss?" came from the back of the car.

"Up here a ways, I need to make a stop," was all he said. His voice was very certain and even. One arm was resting on the car door while his other one was stretched behind the guys sitting in the seat next to him. He reached out and patted a shoulder as they continued. Glances in his direction, checking his certainty, were common on all their outings. He remained steady and often held a smile in his eyes.

"Take a right here," he said. As they approached the corner, an intimidating group of young men hovering there stared them down as they turned. They went about four blocks when he said, "There should be a market on the right side here somewhere. Let's turn in when you see it."

Sure enough, there it was. They turned in, and he said, "If there's a shady spot, try and park there, I'm not sure how long we'll be." Unfortunately, there wasn't a shady spot, so they went to the far side of the parking lot, against the bordering cinderblock and weed-laden wall, and parked.

The engine was turned off, the music stopped, and for a moment, all was quiet.

"I need some air back here," came immediately from one of the four jammed in the back seat.

"Seriously," complained another.

"It must be 100 degrees in here already!" griped the next.

He didn't move, though, or attempt to get out. Instead he said, "Keep the radio going, I'm not sure how long we'll be here. And, roll down the windows," he instructed.

No one was wearing what would be best on a day like this; instead they all wore suits and ties. They were on their way to an evening speaking engagement, featuring their fearless leader. Sweat was already coming down the faces of most of them at this point.

"What? How long do you think we can sit here?" from the one with the short fuse. Cautionary glances were exchanged among several of them. Some were more willing to express their doubt than others.

"Okay, relax guys. Why don't you all go and get some lunch, find a cool place to eat, and come back for me in an hour or so," he suggested.

"I don't know if you've noticed, but it's not the best neighborhood to be killing time in. How about if some of us stay with you," came a concerned suggestion from the one sitting next to him.

"Another time that might fit. But, I need to be here on my own this time." Another pat on the shoulder. "You all go, get some food, and when you come back we'll be ready to continue south for a great evening together," he said. He quickly opened the car door, patted all within reach a quick good-bye, and jogged around to the driver's window. "I think

I saw some food when we got off the freeway. Take the guys there."

He turned and walked toward the market. Before entering, he paused and looked to his left and right, and caught site of a bench to the left of the doors. He walked over, took off his suit jacket, laid it on the back of the bench, and sat down in the full sun.

"He's going to bake out there!" again from the back.

"He knows that, let's go. Get the AC blasting!" And so, they backed out, and passed him once again as they left the parking lot. He waved and smiled as they passed, and yelled out, "Enjoy!"

"What could he have to do here?" asked the guy in the passenger's front seat. "It's the middle of the day, there's hardly anyone here, and those that are here don't even speak English!"

"Who knows?"

"I can't imagine."

"No idea," was all they could say as they drove off and left him sitting on the bench.

✳

"Chia! How are you?" It was one of my few friends left in the city. I'd gone to high school with her, and we had known one another since.

"What's wrong, Celeste? You look terrible," she said.

"Yeah, I just saw Miguel," I said.

"Oh, I'm sorry. Want to get a cold drink?" she asked.

As we sat in the shop, I listened to miserable stories of Chia's life, which wasn't in much better shape than my own. Time slipped away, and I was startled to notice the hour, "I've got to go. I'll see you later, huh? Thanks for the drink," I called back to her as I ran out the door.

I was too late to get the other things the kids needed, so I decided to try and get some water from the outdoor dispensers at the market a few blocks away. As I walked by the various storefronts, the security gates along the sidewalks were being pulled down. The neighborhood was entirely Mexican, and the market area, particularly in the heat of summer, followed the tradition of siesta, closing business for a few hours each afternoon. I could hear people exchanging "Ciao," "See you this evening," "Hasta luego!"

It must have been over 100 degrees. The temperature combined with the bags I was carrying felt unbearable all of the sudden. I was trying to figure out how to get out of the heat once I'd gotten the water. *I can catch the bus near the market, but I'll probably have to wait a while.*

I turned the corner and saw the front of the old market: "Comida Economico" said the sign, with the "d" missing. People were filtering out, as the last minutes of the afternoon's business were winding down. There was no shade on the storefront. There was a bench, which caught my attention, off to the left side, where I was heading for water.

There, by the dispenser, was a man sitting on the bench. He looked like a lawyer or someone in business. He was white and dressed in a really nice suit. I couldn't remember the last time I saw someone like him in our neighborhood. It was not only odd seeing him sitting there in the mid-day heat, but also odd that he was alone and didn't seem to be preparing to go anywhere anytime soon.

He looked up at me as I approached the machine and smiled slightly. I quickly looked down. The only time I'd interacted with white men was when I was serving them a meal at a restaurant or cleaning their houses, and even then, I spoke mostly with their wives or girlfriends while they were in the room.

I pulled one of my empty water containers out of my bag and began to unscrew the lid. I was dripping sweat off my forehead and wiping it off with the back of my hand when I thought I heard him say something. I continued to put the container in place, and he spoke up, "Will you get me a drink of water?"

I looked around and behind me. No one. I glanced at him and returned to filling my bottles. *I must have misunderstood him.*

"Please, will you get me a drink of water?" he clearly said this time, eliciting my response.

"Did you say something?" I asked, stalling while I groped to understand his question.

"Yes," he said, "I asked you if you would get me a drink

of water." I stood motionless taking this in.

Why is he talking to me? Why is he asking me this? Of course I could get him a drink, but why is he asking me to, when he could do this for himself?

The silence grew awkward. I couldn't stand it any longer, "What is a person like you doing asking me for a drink of water, outside a grocery store, in this God-awful heat? In this neighborhood?" I didn't know where my bitterness was coming from but, with every word, my anger and resentment grew. *Did he expect me to serve him here? Was that it?*

My tone didn't seem to distract him. He appeared to be listening to me. His eyes were clear and looked straight at me while I talked. He was probably feeling sorry for me, and this thought angered me further. He nodded slightly as I finished.

"I'm sorry," he said, "this must be really strange for you. I don't mean to alarm you, but it seems like you're familiar around here and have used a water machine before and might be willing to help me with a drink of water? I don't have a container."

I sighed and reluctantly pulled out my coin purse, to which he pulled out a handful of change and let me choose the 75 cents. I put in the money, filled a small container, and handed it to him.

He took a long drink as I continued filling my bottles. I could see the sweat rolling down his forehead. His eyes were looking up at the sky, and then they closed in pleasure as he finished his drink with a loud gulp. His exhale was followed by a big smile as he leaned back against the bench again.

"Don't you wish that water like that was always available?" he stared at the half-filled container in his hand now.

I had no reply. *Yes? Maybe? I don't know.*

I wanted to leave now. I pushed on the last lid and looked over to the bus stop across the street. The bench next to the post was all taped off and had a sign on it saying, "Wet Paint." The surface was glistening in the sun, confirming that I couldn't sit there.

"I've often thought about it," he continued, "why we need so much water. You know?" I didn't. I only looked and stared at him. "I mean, all of us need to drink over and over again, just to stay alive."

A couple came out of the store just then, carrying their groceries. They glanced at me, then at the man. When they saw him, they slowed down and took a longer look. He was out of place, and their response was full of curiosity followed quickly by respect as they looked away.

I began gathering my things to go, forcing and shoving my containers and belongings back into my bags. The couple was gone now. He continued watching me with what felt like interest of some sort. I was turning to walk away when I heard him again.

"Can I call you Celeste?" he asked.

One of my bags slipped out of my hand and dropped to the ground. "Who the hell are you?" startled and mad, I raised my voice.

"Your shirt," he pointed, "your name."

I had forgotten that I was wearing an old work shirt from a former job, with my name embroidered on it. I looked down at the stitching for a moment, flashed a conciliatory smile, and then recoiled again. "Why do you need to call me anything? What do you want . . . sir?" The sarcasm of "sir" came out stronger than I intended.

Two women came out just then, having finished their shopping, chatting and laughing. When they saw us, they stopped talking. I quickly looked down. They passed in silence, looking back and staring a couple of times. I picked up my bag that dropped, and decided to go sit on the curb across the street in front of the wet bench, and wait for the bus there. I didn't want to talk to this man anymore. *Maybe I'm getting dehydrated.*

As I sat down, I looked over and saw the store owner come out, lock the door, nod a brief greeting in the man's direction, and quickly walk away. The lot was now vacant, the sun was at its peak, and all I wanted was for the bus to show up.

Just then, the man stood up and began walking toward me. "Celeste, do you know what I mean?" he called over.

"What?" I snapped. "What you mean about what?" Again, raising my voice.

He went on, seeming not to notice as he continued walking my way, "About water and drinking. It gets tiring to always thirst. It just seems like something's missing," he trailed off as he slowly sat on the curb across the street facing me, leaning forward with his elbows on his knees, looking down. Although an expensive suit and shoes, I noticed his socks were mismatched slightly. One brown: one black. I smiled inwardly at this.

After I said nothing for a while, he looked up again, questioning me with his eyebrows, waiting for me to say something.

"I don't know. It's just part of life you know. So what if we get tired? It's just the way it is," I reasoned. My shirt was beginning to soak through and stick to my skin, and the backs of my knees were dripping now.

"Well, you know what I think? I don't think it has to be that way," he said. I looked up at him. "I think you're tired, Celeste."

I wanted to get up and run, but I was so hot. I looked around. There was nowhere to go. I felt my shoulders curl forward. He was speaking too personally with me. I didn't like it.

"Who are you?" I stayed looking away, pretending to have little interest.

"I have the same question for you. Who are you?" he asked.

Thinking he was being sarcastic, I exhaled a shallow laugh, and looked at him, ready to lash out. But, his eyes told me that he was not being sarcastic, but sincere.

"Who am I?" I asked. He nodded. *Who am I?*

"I'm . . . " I looked up at the sky shaking my head, "I'm . . . not anybody. I'm just someone who got you a drink on a hot day, just getting by." I pulled my hair back away from my face, as sweat dropped from my chin.

"Not true," he said.

I gave a hard look at him now. *He doesn't know anything about me.* "Yes, it is. There's not much more to it," I said sharply.

He just smiled slightly and took a moment to look away himself.

I tried again and began after a deep breath, "I'm a mother; I'm a wife; I'm a poor Mexican-American woman living in a poor neighborhood of South Central LA, trying to get shopping done, with money that I don't have, for my kids at home." My eyes began to water. "And so, yes, I'm tired," my throat was closing, catching me off-guard. I looked down at my old shoes, noticing a worn spot starting to rip where the canvas met the rubber sole.

"I'm sorry, Celeste. Maybe I should let you go home and get back to your kids and your husband," he said easily. I looked up to see some boys who were grouped together on their bikes down on the corner about a half a block away. Each had a cold drink in their hands, as they laughed together. I heard a horn honk from somewhere in the neighborhood.

I looked back down at my shoes. "I don't have a husband," I said in a low voice.

It was quiet. Really quiet.

"I know," he said evenly.

Everything stopped. I was staring aimlessly at the street in the middle of us. My breathing was shallow. Although sweating, I had a rush of chills.

I drew myself together and looked at him, "What do you think you know?"

He called back, held my gaze, and said again, "I know that you have no husband."

The boys on the corner were wheeling away on their bikes, and now, other than an old truck driving by at the nearby intersection, we were the only ones in sight.

I stood up, leaving my bags at the curb, and walked across the street to where he was. "Do you know my friend, Chia? Or, do you work at one of my children's schools? What do you think you know about me?" I was mad. I couldn't piece this together. Fear was creeping up all around.

He looked up and said, "I just know. I know that you've had many husbands, five to be exact, and the man you were with last night, is not your husband at all."

I stepped back, and then took two or three more steps backwards. I looked down. His words were circling all around me, closing me in. I couldn't think of any reason that I would ever talk about this with anyone, or acknowledge what he had just said, with anyone. If I could've crawled into a hole and died right then and there, I would have.

I looked around. Where could I get away? Where

could I hide? The store was closed. The bus wasn't here. I felt hollow. I turned and hurried back to my bags, picked them up, passed back by him and into the parking, returning back the way I'd come. *Maybe I can make it back to Chia's house.*

I began to gasp to catch my breath. A salty drip of tears fell into my mouth. I wiped my cheek with my forearm that was carrying two heavy water jugs in a bag. I couldn't see well. The bag dropped off my arm. I crouched down to try and get my breath in the middle of the parking lot.

Without hearing him approach, I felt his hand on my shoulder, and I heard his knees pop as he lowered down beside me.

"It's okay, Celeste. It'll be okay," he whispered.

"No, it's not!" I cried out, "It's not okay. Nothing is okay." Tears were steady. My nose was dripping.

His fingertips were gentle on my shoulder.

"Why are you here?" I drew in a quivering breath. "What do you want from me?" I was barely able to say.

"I want to help you," he said simply.

"How are you going to help me?" I nearly spit as I spoke.

"Well, I don't know if this will make sense, but, only someone who really sees, can really help," he said.

I wiped my eyes again. He offered me his handkerchief, and I wiped my nose. I couldn't look up. I was dizzy.

"And so," he continued, "I really see you, and I have for a long, long time,"

"What are you talking about?" I kept my eyes down,

folding the handkerchief for the other side.

"I remember when this started for you." He paused for a moment. He seemed to be considering something. My heart was racing. I panicked and reached for one of my bags and tried to get my footing to stand back up and leave.

He reached out to take my hand in his, very gently, squeezing my fingers in his surrounding hold. I stopped. He slowly began, "I remember your First Communion, and your parents' fighting. I remember your father's anger and the abuse in your home."

My eyes began to sting again, my heart was beating outside my chest, "You what?"

He continued, "I remember Jose."

At this, I pulled my hand out of his and clasped my hands up to my chest, turning my shoulders away from him.

"Don't Celeste. Don't pull away from me," he pleaded kindly, and softly.

Just then, I heard the sound of an approaching car turning into the parking lot and looked up. "Is everything okay?" asked a young man in the front passenger seat, as he pulled up near us. The car was packed, all with men, in dress shirts and ties. They all had looks on their faces of concern and curiosity. I looked away quickly and covered my face.

"Will you wait for me over across the lot, and I'll finish up here and be over in a minute?" he asked them. There was a pause.

"Okay, we'll be over there," said the young man's voice,

and they pulled slowly away. I could hear the window go up and their whispers beginning.

I took a deep breath and stood up, "You can go now. Your friends are waiting. Thank you for your help." I was leaning away and reaching again for my bags.

"Celeste, you need to know what I know. You need to see what I see," he said as he stood.

"I don't want to know what else you know," I said as I looked into his eyes shaking my head. "You're scaring me."

"You don't need to be afraid of me. I really mean it when I say that the one who sees you, is the one who can help you," he repeated. His hand touched my shoulder again, and I felt myself give in slightly.

He continued as I waited there, "I know about your life, about your children, about your divorces."

Shame overwhelmed me. Without knowing it, I was curling into a ball, head tucked, shoulders hunched, involuntarily lowering myself to the ground again. I couldn't face this. I suddenly began hearing myself moan really low.

Please no more. Please don't say anymore or say out loud what happened, I cried out silently inside.

"I was at the clinic that day, and I was at the church when you went to confess," his words felt like cuts on my skin, slicing through my secrets.

I couldn't take it. I fell over on my side onto the hot pavement, curled up, and wept, drawing my knees into my chest. I knew the men in the car could probably hear me now, but it didn't matter anymore. He knew everything about me. "Oh God, oh God," I sobbed, over and over.

He bent over and with his long, strong arms, wrapped around me, securely picked me up and off of the scalding surface. He steadied me onto my feet and into his chest, bracing me up. "I'm here," he was saying. "I'm right here."

Several minutes passed, of just this. Me sobbing, and him saying, "It's alright. I'm here. I'm with you." Then I heard him whisper, "It didn't happen right." His arms felt massive and circled both my shoulders, holding me from the side. I felt his chin rest on my head, as his arms pulled me in a bit more, holding me.

"You missed out, Celeste," he whispered again.

"What?" I barely spoke through my tears.

"The priest that day when you went to confess so long ago."

I quieted my crying, trying to hold my body still enough to hear him.

"When you asked him for forgiveness and his response was to separate you. You're not separated, Celeste. I forgive you," his voice cracked. *Was he crying?*

He cleared his throat and took a deep breath, "Celeste, I want you to stop hiding from this and lying to yourself about the pain in your life." I felt one of his arms slip away for a moment, wiping his face, and then back around me. "I want life for you, Celeste. I want you to know you're forgiven, and I want you to stop living in such a shattered way, filling your life with things that keep hurting you and keeping your life broken. Do you hear me, Celeste?" he asked.

I couldn't move. I stared vacantly at the black surface of the parking lot.

"Do you hear me, Celeste?" he asked again, shaking me a little.

I could only nod. My body was frozen. I then reached up and was clenching my hands over his arms, around me. My fingernails were nearly digging into his skin.

Hold me up, hold me up! I was pleading inside.

I could hear and feel his breath. I backed my head away enough to look up into his eyes. I suddenly felt I had to see him.

His tear-filled eyes looked down into my searching eyes. Full. Knowing.

Although I couldn't speak, I could hear my heart say loudly in my chest: *Yes. I hear you.*

I closed my eyes and leaned heavy and slowly into his chest and felt his full embrace close me in.

I hear you now. Yes, I hear you.

Just then, I felt a smile begin to spread, as if it were my first. I began to pat his embracing arms around me.

"Thank you. Thank you," I took a deep breath and loudly exhaled, "Thank you."

Epilogue

I showed up at Chia's the next morning after getting the kids to school.

"Hi. Come on in," she said opening her door, while wiping her hands on a dishtowel. "What's the occasion? Did you have more trouble with Miguel after I saw you?" she asked with concern.

I walked over to her kitchen table and slowly sat down. I looked at her. She looked at me with a questioning face, "Well? Are you okay?"

"Yes, I'm fine," I said.

"Do you want a cup of coffee? Or have you eaten? You're so quiet. What's wrong, Celeste?" she came to the table and touched my shoulder.

"Chia, sit down with me," I pointed to the chair across from me.

"You're worrying me. What's wrong?" she continued.

"Chia, something happened to me yesterday, after I saw you," I said.

"Oh, honey, what happened, are you okay?" she worried and put her hands over mine.

"Yes, I'm okay. In fact, I'm more than okay. I'm maybe

better than I've ever been," I smiled and tears began to fill my eyes.

She smiled, "Sweetie, tell me. Tell me then." She scooted her chair in and set down the towel on the table.

"I met someone," I began. Chia smiled knowingly, tilting her head. "No, no, not like a lover or a friend, but someone different. I had a conversation with him," I took a deep breath.

Chia raised her eyebrows, "Yeah? Well, then tell me."

A note from the author

If you're reading this I'm guessing that you are curious. Maybe curious about where these ideas came from? Maybe you wonder how someone would have the audacity to suggest some of the possibilities of the stories and characters in the previous pages?

The ideas? The characters? The audacity?

The inspiration for this book has been to heighten the valuable moments when we receive the message of love and freedom in the stories and conversations of Jesus. I have felt led in an unusual way to allow my characters, their circumstances, their dialogue, and their decisions to work together in whatever fashion I can create, to best orchestrate a spotlight on freedom, love, and needed forgiveness and for this to be as relevant as possible; first for me, and then hopefully for you.

My English literature teacher my junior year taught us that God is outside of time (she was a retired nun teaching in a large public high school). He created time. So he's not limited to expressing himself in one century or in one culture or only in the past. Maybe he's expressing himself now? Maybe he's expressing himself in New York in the financial world, or in a poor Los Angeles neighborhood, maybe in Brazil, or in the Bay Area of San Francisco? And I don't mean figuratively or theoretically, but literally, actually … now.

In *The Story of Cole Carson* (from the story of *The Rich Young Ruler* in Mark 10), I rely heavily on Jesus' words that seem to simply trail-off at the end of the scene . . . "All things are possible with God." This has always made me wonder about the possibility of God's continued activity in the man's life after this scene, just like Jonathan Sanders' continued impact in Cole Carson's life.

In *Thirsty* (from the story of *The Woman of Samaria* in John 4), the historical woman has always been too easy for me to dismiss because of her seemingly promiscuous lifestyle and disregard for marriage. However, we've never really known her story. Everyone has a story, right? There's always a story behind our actions, and Celeste is no different. Her loneliness and need to be noticed and loved has finally caught up with her when the Jesus character meets her at the water dispenser in front of the grocery story on a very hot day in Los Angeles.

Finally, in *The Long Road* (from the story that Jesus told about the lost son in Luke 15) the return and welcome of Jacob, the son who left, has always caused me to wonder about the unique power of love and freedom that God offers. The father's response to both sons is by far one of the most powerful revelations in Jesus' life on earth. Through this story, Jesus essentially dismantles the existing rules of religion at the time and introduces a new story, a larger story, and more compelling story of love.

Through the father's response, we see that God's heart has room for us all: those who leave and those who stay. He's saying his love is without limits or parameters. A non-discriminant love like this is too beautiful for words. It's an invitation we'll not find anywhere else. This is too good to be true in our world.

Or is it?

Is it possible that no one has it right but God himself, and that this is what Jesus was trying to describe?

Is there a home to return to? Is there a father waiting? Can we imagine that some of our attitudes and actions aren't setting us free, that our leaving needs to stop, and that wholeness, freedom, and restoration await us in his love?

Does God's love call the liar home? Does God's love wait and look for the criminal to return? The addict? The terrorist and the racist? Does God's love reach out to the angry religious activists, the judgmental, and the self-righteous? Does God's love embrace the immoral? The counterfeit? The determined atheist? Those of us who tear apart or disregard a family or a marriage? The abuser? What about the self-indulgent? The corrupt?

And, what about me? What about you?

Is there a home and father waiting for us? Can he handle all of this, love us, and enable us to be set free? As we come in touch with his disarming love and wholeness . . . can we finally stay?

Could he be saying <u>this</u> to us?

"You still belong."

Looking closely at the life of Jesus will always bring challenging, rewarding, and unbelievable conclusions, as well as new possibilities. This could keep your book club busy for a good long while. And, I hope that it does.

Bless you and enjoy!
Jamie Lisea

Richthirstyhungry.com
Jamielisea.com

Acknowledgements

There are too many friends, who have deeply encouraged me along the way, to thank them all. I'm so grateful for your generosity and kindness, which have given me the courage, strength, and support I've needed to try, explore, create, lead, and follow.

There are, however, a few specific partners who I must acknowledge.

Thank you Scott Lisea and Ginger Hendrix, my two most consistent cheerleaders along the way. I don't think this would have become a reality without your honest feedback peppered with huge doses of belief in me.

Thank you Emily De La Llave, Emily Parker, Hillary Hope, and Krystina Montemurro from The Creative Arcade who researched, edited, designed, and formatted my words and vision into the book you are reading now. Each of you were so patient and gentle with someone so new to this. I'm sure I asked exasperating things of you, and yet you never said so.

Thank you Tyler Lisea for taking the author photo for the back cover. "Good job," says your mother.

Thank you Marge Petersen for confirming the life in these stories by listening so intently as I read them aloud to you. Your smile and the wonder in your eyes helped me realize that we were experiencing the stories afresh. I love being in awe of God, together.

Thank you dear Ron and Lee Hanna, for fostering in me, 25 years ago, a curiosity and hunger for the possibilities of God. Your open invitation to the Lord to creatively reveal

Himself to you has inspired me. I want to be just like you when I grow up.

Finally, thank you Mom and Dad for staying married, for putting your hope in the Lord just before I arrived, and for loving me so well. I am forever grateful to you.